A Clan M

# THE FORBIDDEN

# *Highlander*

## *Also available from*
# *Terri Brisbin*

### A HIGHLAND FEUDING Series:
Stolen by the Highlander
The Highlander's Runaway Bride
Kidnapped by the Highland Rogue
Claiming His Highland Bride
A Healer for the Highlander
The Highlander's Inconvenient Bride – crossover with the
CLAN MACLERIE series
Her Highlander for One Night

### UNEXPECTED HEIRS OF SCOTLAND series:
The Lady Takes It All
A Lady's Agreement

### The MACKENDIMEN CLAN Series:
A Love Through Time
Once Forbidden
A Highlander's Hope (novella)
A Matter of Time

### WARRIORS OF THE STONE CIRCLES Series:
Rising Fire
Raging Sea
Blazing Earth

### The STORM Series:
A Storm of Passion
A Storm of Love novella
A Storm of Pleasure
Mistress of the Storm

### The CLAN MACLERIE Series:
Taming the Highlander
Surrender to the Highlander
Possessed by the Highlander
Taming The Highland Rogue
The Highlander's Stolen Touch

At The Highlander's Mercy
The Forbidden Highlander in HIGHLANDERS
The Highlander's Dangerous Temptation
Yield to The Highlander
The Highlander's Inconvenient Bride – crossover with A
Highland Feuding series!
Her Highlander for One Night

## Related stories (same clan 500 years later)
The Earl's Secret
Blame It On The Mistletoe in ONE CANDLELIT
CHRISTMAS

## The DUMONT Series:
The Dumont Bride
The Norman's Bride
The Countess Bride
Love at First Step from THE CHRISTMAS VISIT
The King's Mistress
The Claiming of Lady Joanna from THE BETROTHAL

## The KNIGHTS of BRITTANY Series:
A Night for Her Pleasure
The Conqueror's Lady
The Mercenary's Bride
His Enemy's Daughter

## STAND-ALONE STORIES:
The Queen's Man
The Duchess's Next Husband
The Maid of Lorne
Kidnapping the Laird
What The Duchess Wants – for newsletter
subscribers only!
Upon A Misty Skye
Across A Windswept Isle
A Traitor's Heart in BRANDYWINE BRIDES
The Storyteller – A Ghosts of Culloden Moor Novella
An Outlaw's Honor ~ A Midsummer Knights romance
Tempted by Her Viking Enemy
The Highlander's Substitute Wife (HIGHLAND LLIANCES

A Clan MacLerie Novella

# THE FORBIDDEN

USA TODAY BESTSELLING AUTHOR

# *The Forbidden Highlander*

Cover Design by Dar Albert
WickedSmartDesigns.com

Formatting by Nina Pierce
Nina@NinaPierce.com

ISBN 978-1-949425-13-0

LUCKENBOOTH**PRESS**

# ONE

*Scottish Highlands*
*1370 A.D.*

It was only a touch of his hand, the slightest and briefest of touches, and forbidden, but Elizabeth desired it. Glancing up, she met his gaze and saw something there she dared not to hope she would see. Her throat tightened and her mouth dried, no words able to come out.

"Elizabeth," he whispered as he rubbed his thumb along the inside of her palm.

The sound of her name on his lips sent shivers and chills through her body and brightened her heart. Elizabeth MacLerie enjoyed the sensations for the moment, knowing that none of it could continue.

Their game of chess complete, he stood from the stool and stepped away from the table, waiting for her to follow. And, damn her heart, she did. Trying to let nothing of her nervousness show to those whom she—they—passed, Elizabeth understood that something had changed between her and James in that momentary caress.

A line had been crossed, one they both knew should not be breached. But, with only a touch of his hand and a whisper of her name, they had.

She had been in love before, just once, and it had come upon her like a storm—with wildness and breathlessness and foolishness and danger. This time, love had crept up on her, surprising her with its quiet, silent approach. Though, this time as that, the danger remained a constant.

Elizabeth followed James, hoping to speak to him, but his father called to him and she watched as he joined his parents and Ciara Robertson in some discussion.

Elizabeth now knew what heaven and hell were like—she was living them both. Glancing across the clearing and meeting his gaze, she saw the possibilities of both in his blue eyes as they each paused for a moment before looking away.

Her heart pounded and her body ached every time they spoke. His calm manner and deliberate actions appealed to that part of her that wished to avoid any of the melodrama that had threatened her happiness and her place in her family just a year before. His polite and careful approach to her, never overstepping, never demanding, promised that life with him would find her content and happy. Now on the road, journeying back to her home in Lairig Dubh and spending so much time in his company, she could convince herself of everything working out in her favor.

She could hope.

All it took, though, was one glance across the clearing to show her that she'd really entered the realms of hell. James Murray was betrothed and contracted to marry her closest friend, Ciara Robertson, and not her. Elizabeth was the first to look away, as Ciara claimed his attention once more.

His betrothed.

Her closest friend.

If she had looked away at that moment, she would have missed the glance Ciara threw in another direction. Elizabeth did not have to turn to know who stood in the shadows at the edge of the camp. The expression that flitted across Ciara's face just then, a mix of longing and love and loss, meant that Tavis MacLerie watched them even as she did.

It would not surprise Elizabeth to hear the stern voice of Father Micheil echoing through the clearing and warning all of them about the cost of the sins they so eagerly committed and would so eagerly commit if given the chance. But the one thing that held them back and kept all their wayward, sinful longings—each for someone not meant to be theirs—under control was honor.

Ciara had broken off a number of betrothals and she was, Elizabeth understood, determined to follow through with this one. Not because she loved James, for she did not, but to uphold her promise to her parents and the others depending on this marriage and the benefits it brought to two families and other allies.

James was the heir of his father and William Murray needed this advantageous marriage to rebuild his family's holdings and to make alliances with the powerful MacLerie and Robertson clans. James understood the realities that required this marriage, no matter where his heart wished to go.

Tavis MacLerie had buried one wife and had counted Ciara as a friend, never realizing that her true feelings had little to do with remaining his friend. Elizabeth had lived through every stage of their relationship, from the tumultuous heartbreak when Ciara asked him to marry her and he refused her, to the day she accepted James's offer of marriage and giving up any hope of marrying Tavis. Though now, from one look at his face, Elizabeth knew he regretted that he had not accepted her offer and her love, for he loved Ciara even if he did not admit it.

So, instead of following their hearts, each of them would honor their loyalties and commitments. Each of them would end up married to someone they did not love, all for the sake of honor and duty.

Elizabeth recognized that even if James were free to marry, she would not be the woman his parents sought for a marriage. Her parents would offer a small dowry and she had not the elevated connections and relatives that Ciara offered.

And, if word of her disgrace from a year ago got out, her shame would keep her from being his. Though Connor had promised to protect her reputation, she worried every day that her behavior and the results would come to light. If James's parents learned of her fall from grace, they would never allow her to become their son's wife.

With so much of the outcome inevitable, Elizabeth decided to enjoy the few moments that they could snatch away and to remember them...and him always. The following days' travel provided her with several special moments, ones she would hold in her breaking heart.

But, when they all reached Lairig Dubh, Elizabeth understood the way things would be, even if her heart refused to accept it.


*Lairig Dubh*
*Lands of the MacLerie clan*

When his amber eyes flashed with anger, James Murray could well understand why Connor MacLerie was still called the Beast of the Highlands. And unfortunately, the Beast's ire was aimed directly at James.

"These questions are coming very late into things, would you not say, James?" The calm tone of the laird's voice did nothing to assuage James's sense of impending doom.

Connor rose then, walked to the large window that faced the yard and stood silent for a few moments. James felt the urge to confess all manner of sins during that silence, but he held his words behind his teeth and waited on the laird. The less said, the fewer transgressions revealed.

"If you have concerns about your upcoming nuptials, just know that many marriages face less than auspicious beginnings," he said without facing James. "My own, for example, to Lady Jocelyn."

A subtle description for an event known across the Highlands and most of the Lowlands as well. Having had, as the story went, killed his first wife for not giving him a son, Connor MacLerie forced marriage on Jocelyn MacCallum in exchange for her brother's life. Inauspicious would not have been the word James would choose to describe that situation, but he did not challenge Connor's choice.

"Ciara Robertson would not seem too hard a burden for a man to bear. She is lovely, well-spoken, educated, amiable...and wealthy. Most men would fight for her hand in marriage," Connor said as he turned to face James now. "Before you take any actions, you must be certain about the path you are taking. Have you considered the cost to your family? To your reputation? To the lass?"

Was he certain? Could he break the betrothal and face all the ramifications of that action? Would he place Elizabeth in danger of sharing whatever sanctions would face him in this? He was about to nod when the laird asked the pivotal and most revealing question of him.

"There is a woman involved?"

Could Connor read his thoughts? James had shared more details of his quandary with Lady Jocelyn but not with Connor. She'd suggested he speak with the laird to see what could be done. Dare he confess it all to the man who could destroy everything with but a word?

"Elizabeth," James said quietly before meeting that intimidating gaze once more. Then, he said her name once more making it a declaration for the first time. "Elizabeth MacLerie."

"Ciara's closest friend?" Connor asked. James winced at the tone now in the laird's voice as he nodded.

He took no pleasure in knowing that he would hurt Ciara. Truth be told, she was a fetching lass. Intelligent. Skilled in numbers and languages. Trained by the best— her stepfather—to understand financial matters. A gift to the man who would marry her. But during their journey back here to her home, back here to their wedding, his heart had been stolen by another.

Elizabeth was the perfect foil to Ciara—auburn hair to her fair, talkative to her quietude, practical to her well-schooled, and in love with him when Ciara loved another. It had taken him longer than it had taken her to realize the feelings that grew between them and the strength of those feelings. Now though, after watching the growing misery in his betrothed's eyes as their marriage approached and knowing his own, he knew he must take action. No matter the cost.

"Aye, Ciara's friend. Laird, it was not something we planned—"

"I did not think that," Connor said sharply. "Elizabeth knows you are here? Speaking to me about this matter?"

Ah, therein lay the problem—he had not consulted Elizabeth yet. They'd spoken of their feelings in hushed tones during the dark of night when they could manage some time together. Or other times during the journey here. He had not pulled his courage together until this morn, with the wedding swiftly approaching.

"I..." He could not think of how to answer. Connor held up his hand to stop him.

"I cannot make this decision for you and will not make it easy for you to do so, either," Connor said as he sat once more. "There will be problems, serious and possibly deadly effects of choosing to ignore your duty to your family and to your honor, James. If my softhearted wife led you to believe I would support you in this, you should know that she was mistaken."

James's stomach clenched at the strong words in spite of having considered all those things before stepping foot in this chamber. The lady's words had sounded promising, or mayhap he had simply heard what he wanted to hear?

"Other men have faced this same conundrum and made their own choices—as you must."

Connor stood and strode to the door of his chamber. The discussion was done. Connor MacLerie, the MacLerie and the Earl of Douran, had heard him out and would do no more. James wondered, though...

"Will you speak of this to my parents?" he asked.

"What would I tell them? You came seeking my counsel. No more, no less."

With nothing more to say, James left the chamber. He had duties to see to and things to accomplish, but more than that, he had a decision to make. As he left the keep and considered his next step, he knew his mind and his decision had been made already.

Now, if only Elizabeth would agree.

# Two

Elizabeth MacLerie paced the small clearing, trying to sort out her feelings and thoughts over the matter of her and James. The guilt in her heart grew each time she looked at him and thought of her closest friend. So much so that she considered going to speak to Father Micheil and confess sins of pride and, worse, coveting and lust, to the holy man. Pushing her hair over her shoulder, she glanced once again down the path for James.

The scene she'd interrupted yesterday had given her, and her desire for him, pause—it was difficult to watch him embrace and kiss the woman he would marry, especially when that woman was not her, but was her best friend, Ciara. If not for the sadness and guilt in his eyes when their gazes met, she would have refused this meeting. She would have accepted that she would have to force the soft feelings from her heart. He'd begged her to hear him out and so she would. Even if it was the end of her dreams.

They were, the three of them, in a terrible situation where none would end up happy, but where all must carry out their part for the sake of their families and their honor. Ciara, she knew, loved Tavis, but would marry James because of the benefits it would bring to both of their families. James, if his words were true, loved her, but must marry Ciara for the same reasons—family and honor. She loved both her friend and James, and must stand by and watch them wed and face a life of misery watching them make a life together.

It was a hopeless situation that would lead them all to an unhappy life.

She turned at the sound of leaves crunching underfoot and found James there, standing in the shade of a tall tree and staring at her. The serious expression on his face lightened for a brief moment as their gazes met but was back in place when he reached her side. Elizabeth's knees trembled and breathing became difficult as she faced the end of things between them.

James took her hand and lifted it to his mouth, kissing the inside of her wrist and sending shivers through her whole body. She, the one who had counseled Ciara against the need for feeling such things, now fell victim to every sensation that raced through her skin and her blood. He placed another kiss in her palm before entwining their fingers and tugging her along to follow him deeper into the cover of the forest.

Words, the ones she wanted to say and the ones she must, tumbled through her mind as they walked off the path and into the thicker, darker copse that would hide them from sight. Then he stopped and faced her, not releasing her hand. Indeed, he pulled her closer and lowered his mouth to hers. And—damn her!—she lifted hers to accept the kiss. She opened to his tongue and he tasted her deeply. Elizabeth leaned against him, clutching the leather of his jacket with her free hand. When her needy whimper echoed through the trees surrounding them and floated along the glen, she pulled away from him.

Memories of the sight of him kissing and caressing Ciara, much as he did now to her, reminded her of their path. She rubbed the back of her hand across her mouth, trying to stop the urges his kiss caused within her. She looked at him and saw his chest heaving as he breathed deeply and unevenly, his gaze never leaving her face.

"Elizabeth, I can explain," he said, stepping toward her again.

"The kissing? The way you touched her?" She could not help the hurt or jealousy that tinged her voice. She was both and would not hide either from him.

"Aye, all that and more," he said, softly, reaching for her hands. "I have found a husband for you after all."

The tears burned her eyes and her throat. Ciara had

suggested that James find Elizabeth a husband from among his clan so she would stay with them in Perthshire after their marriage. Now, such an offer, coming from him, sounded like blasphemy.

"James, I..." she began. Shaking her head, she tried to form the words.

"Listen to me, Elizabeth," he said, shaking her hands to gain her attention. "Yesterday was a test. I suspected that there were no feelings between Ciara and I and that kiss proved it to me. Her lips, her body, do not cause what yours do."

He pulled her into his arms and kissed her until they both lost their breath. Sliding his hand around until it rested on her buttocks, he pressed her against his body...and the very evident proof of the growing passion between them. She should push him away, but she gave in to the scandalous way he made her feel, rubbing her hips against his strong body. Then, he leaned away, cupping her face in his hands.

"My heart is yours, my sweet Elizabeth," he whispered. His words, his pledge of love, only served to tear her own heart in pieces.

"But, you cannot...we cannot..." He shook his head and kissed her to stop her words. Then he gazed at her once more.

"Marry me."

She froze, blinking several times at the unbelievable words he'd uttered. They were a denial of all they lived by, and she could not get her mind to accept such a thing. As though he understood she could not conceive of such a thing, he repeated them.

"Marry me, Elizabeth. Be my wife."

The moment spun out between them as her heart warred with her mind, even as her heart tried to hope. It could not.

"James, it is worse than folly to think on such things that can never, never be. It is cruel and not something I would expect from you," she accused. Pulling free, she turned so that he could not see the torment that must be visible in her eyes. "You are betrothed to another and not free to make such an offer." No matter how much she wanted him to do so.

"And if I were free? Would you marry me then?"

"Do not ask something like this, James." He strode to her and gathered her in his arms.

"I want to know. Would you?"

It took only a moment to give her answer—the word had been on her tongue since she'd fallen in love with him and only awaited the right time to say it. In spite of the sheer folly and incredible danger of it, the time was now.

"Aye. I would." Saying the words did not lighten the burden on her heart. Instead guilt assailed her for her betrayal of her friend and her duty to her family. "But, it cannot be. It would be best if we ended this now." She took the first step away from him, from the love he offered, and back toward the life she would lead without him.

A clean break, one that began at this moment and extended for the rest of her life would be the only way to salvage her honor and her heart. She would decline Ciara's offer to move with her to Perthshire and be her companion. Since Elizabeth suspected that Ciara had recognized the attraction between her and James, most likely she would not even have to make up some excuse. Her friend would not force her to create a lie to cover the uncomfortable and unforgivable truth between them.

Elizabeth forced one foot to move in front of the other, intent on leaving him now, but his grasp from behind her prevented her from doing so.

"I cannot marry her, not for family nor for honor, when I love you," he said softly. His breath tickled her ear as he spoke. And the words warmed her heart, no matter that he spoke of something that could not be. "I plan to break the betrothal and want you to come with me...away from here."

She faced him and stared into his eyes, trying to determine if his intent was true. All she could see was love shining there.

But Ciara was the bold one. Ciara was the taker of risks, the one to challenge the way things were done and did things that only men did. Not her. Not Elizabeth. With but one exception, one she had learned a dear lesson from, she followed the rules, she did as she was told. How could she agree to something that would break all the rules and would tear apart her family and loyalties?

"Come with you? Your parents will never allow you to do that."

"I am not asking them. Though if you agree to my proposal, you take to husband a man who can claim little more than what he carries and who can promise nothing but the love in his heart."

"Jamie..." she whispered, so tempted to accept his offer. "I canna...we canna...do this." She could remember no one who had betrayed the laird and not lived to regret it. Worse, they would not be the only targets of the earl's fury—his clan and her family would bear it, too. "The laird would..." She could not even think of what Connor MacLerie was capable of doing in retribution for such a public act against his honor. Against his plans.

"Elizabeth, 'tis a simple matter now for me. With your consent, we will leave this night, once the keep and village have settled in."

"This very night, Jamie?" Elizabeth worried her teeth over her lip and shook her head. "'Tis so soon."

"If you have any hesitation, any reason you do not wish to come away with me and be my wife, say it now. I have spent my whole life living for my family's plans and will not continue it now if you will be mine." He smiled then, a slight lift of the corners of his mouth that made it a sad one. "Aye, it must be this night."

She was torn. Torn between accepting his love and forswearing it. Torn between being bold and courageous and being unable to claim the love, and life, he offered. Torn between always being the one to follow the rules and mores and the one to challenge them. Ciara would know what to do. Ciara would...

Instead of answering him with words, she took hold of his shoulders, drew him nearer and kissed him. She knew the moment he understood for that kiss changed to become one of claiming and accepting and a promise. Jamie's strong arms surrounded her and she melded against his body, opening herself to his mouth and his hands. When his palm covered her breast, she moaned against his mouth and shivered in anticipation. He turned his mouth, slanting his lips and taking hers.

Her body remembered the excitement and thrill of passion and blossomed under his touch. Elizabeth arched against him. Sliding her arms around him, she clutched at the back of his jacket and pressed herself tighter to him. His body roared to life at their embrace and she felt the proof of his arousal against her belly. Heat pooled between her legs and her breathing labored as desire for him burned in her blood. When his thumb flicked over the tightened tip of her breast, she wanted to sink to the ground and pull him on top of her.

"Elizabeth," he whispered against her mouth. He kissed her lips and cheeks and then her forehead. Tangling his hands in her hair, he smiled at her as he leaned in to taste her one last time before stepping back and releasing her. "I will make all the arrangements. Go about your day as you planned."

"When will we leave?" she asked, gathering the loosened hair back into a braid. Her body ached for more of him, but this was not the time.

"After the meal in the keep. It will be short and simple fare since there are preparations for the morrow underway." A shadow of guilt flitted across his gaze and was gone in a moment. "Pack only what you will need for a few days and meet me here."

"Ciara has asked me to stay with her this night," she whispered, trying to keep the guilt that assuaged her own heart from showing. Or from stopping their plans.

Jamie smiled at her. "I am certain you can come up with some explanation." He lifted her hand to his mouth. "Now, we must go about our duties for the rest of the day."

Then he said the words that sealed their plan in her heart.

"You have made me the happiest of men, Elizabeth. Your love gives me the courage to claim you as my own."

His lips touched hers in a gentle kiss, one over much too soon and too tame for her taste in this invigorating moment. Jamie stepped away and waited for her to leave first. Her first paces were the hardest, but then the thrill of their plans and the hope for a future together lightened her feet and she found herself racing through the woods. Arms outstretched, she touched the branches and leaves as she passed them, laughing aloud with each step.

Soon, she reached her parents' cottage and Elizabeth paused for a moment. She needed to gather some clothing and supplies and hide them outside. She needed to get back to the keep and attend to Ciara.

Ciara.

And she must deceive her best friend in order to steal Ciara's betrothed....

It was going to be the longest day of her life.

# THREE

The moonlight lit the unfamiliar path as James led the horse along it. He had walked this way several times since arriving here in Lairig Dubh, never dreaming that it would be his escape route. Though he understood all the dangers and the repercussions of the actions they took now, each step grew lighter and more decisive.

Glancing ahead and behind to make certain no one followed or knew of his plan, he made his way to the place they'd met before and held his breath. Staring into the shadows of the copse of trees, he watched as a slim figure moved and became visible to him.

"Elizabeth," he whispered, as she drew closer. Her smaller hand slipped into his and he squeezed it. "I hoped... I hoped."

At first glance, it appeared that she wore sensible

garments, but as his gaze moved down to her legs now encased in a man's trews, his body tightened in response. Had she any idea of the man he became around her? Or the effect she had on his ability to think logically? He was throwing aside his heritage, his name and possibly his life to have her and none of it worried him now that she was in his grasp.

"What now?" she whispered back.

"We must be on our way. With the full moon above and clear weather for once, we can be miles away before morning."

He secured the bag she held to the saddle and then mounted. Holding his hand down to her, he helped her mount behind him. Once she had settled, and as he tried to ignore her legs against his, he urged the horse on with his knees.

James had studied maps of the area owned by Connor and drawn his own, planning a journey that would follow part of the same path they'd taken from the south. Once nearer to the coast, they would go east along the borders to reach the lands of a distant cousin, where they could stay while making plans. He had coin to buy what they needed along the way.

The silence of the night surrounded them as they rode farther and farther away from Lairig Dubh. Only the sound of the horse's hooves along the beaten dirt path or the occasional night bird or owl broke the quiet. Each minute moved them further from their old life and toward their new one.

When the road changed pitch or angle, Elizabeth's hands tightened around his waist, sometimes her fingers would grab hold of the fabric of his cloak. She shifted once or twice, bringing her more in contact with him, so close that he could feel her heart pounding against his back. Or mayhap that was his own? After riding for some time, James knew he needed to give Elizabeth a break.

He eased them to a slower pace and then let the horse walk a distance to cool down. Once he drew to a halt, he slid off and reached up to help Elizabeth down. His hands spanned her waist with ease, but the contact of her legs sliding down his made his grasp a tenuous one. When her face was level to his, he leaned in and kissed her. Her reaction surprised him, for she wrapped her arms and legs around him and opened to him. All manner of images filled his brain even as blood raced through his body, readying it to claim her.

This was not his intention when he stopped their journey, but, hell, she was his and she was in his arms. He slid his arms around her, holding her tightly against him while he savored the feel of her lovely curves. She was his and his alone. He tasted her deeply and took in the soft moan of pleasure that echoed in the silence around them. With each touch of their mouths, her hold on him and his on her tightened and their bodies melded in an imitation of how they would join their flesh. When a cold wind rustled the trees around them and reminded James of both the lateness and the miles yet ahead of them, he lifted his head and smiled at her.

"You tempt me to folly, lass," he whispered as he eased her down to stand. "Clouds gather." He nodded above to where the thickening clouds began to shroud the full moon...and its light. "If you can still ride, we should cover whatever distance we can before the weather breaks."

"I can," Elizabeth said. At first she glanced away but then she met his gaze once more. "You tempt me as well, James."

For a man who'd planned to live his life by making practical choices and decisions, he'd given himself over to passion and desire's control very quickly. Filled with anticipation of their future together, James reluctantly released her.

"See to your needs, Elizabeth. And then we'll be on our way."

"Where are we going?" she asked. "This looks like the road we took back from Perth."

"It is. We'll follow this until we reach the road that heads south to Glasgow. There is a small village near there...and a priest who will marry us."

"How did you find it?" she asked, smiling at him in a way that warmed his heart.

"I noticed the village as we passed through it. When I decided I...we must elope, I asked about it."

"Wasn't that dangerous?"

"Lady MacLerie seemed very forthcoming in her suggestions."

"The lady knows about us?" Elizabeth gasped. "About this?"

"Although I did not tell her specifically, but aye, I believe she knows what I planned to do. She spoke about a cousin of the earl's who was married by a priest of the Old Church." He smiled, now realizing how detailed the lady's directions were to him. "No one knows anything about our plans—yet. I left a note behind to explain, but it will not be found until morning. So, we are safe for now."

She nodded and turned from him then and he watched as her long legs, encased in and outlined by the trews she wore, carried her away from him. He might have even taken a step after her before he realized she needed some privacy. Laughing, he turned back and checked the saddle and bags tied in place, looking for some of the food he'd packed.

Elizabeth finished her task and found Jamie waiting for her where she'd left him. He held out a chunk of bread to her and she nodded her thanks as she took it. Her stomach had churned through most of the day, including the midday meal at the keep and the dinner that her mother had made, so it did not surprise her when it now grumbled with hunger.

"I did not eat much today," she admitted to him. "I was too nervous after speaking to you."

"Here, have this, too, then," he said, holding out a small piece of yellow cheese and another chunk of bread. "You will need your strength." Their gazes met as she thought about what was ahead of them. The guilty expression that filled his blue eyes told her they thought on different matters.

She accepted the proffered food without comment and ate it all. By the time she'd swallowed the last bite, he held out a skin of ale to her and she drank some. Then, he stored everything in their bags and mounted first. She grasped his hand and pulled herself up behind him, easing her body into position so as to not startle the horse. Elizabeth gathered her cloak around her and slid her arms around his waist to steady herself as they rode.

In truth, she liked riding like this.

She could embrace him, feeling the strength of his muscles beneath her hands and arms as they rode. With her legs pressed against his came a new awareness of heat between them. She'd shamelessly pilfered a pair of her brother's trews, believing that it would be easier to travel unnoticed in them. She never considered the pleasure of holding Jamie between them.

As they crossed the miles through the night, she fell asleep against his back, clutching his cloak to hold on and enjoying the heat of his body against her. He even held onto her hands to keep her secure as they rode. They interrupted their journey for a few, brief stops—always seeing to their comfort and traveling on. Then, not long after the first light of dawn began to brighten the skies above, thunder echoed above them, warning of approaching storms.

The first drops of rain did not bother them, but as it turned into torrents, Jamie guided the horse to a slower and safer pace and finally brought them to a halt under a thick copse of trees. Even the meager shelter offered there was better than nothing and they waited a short time, hoping the rains would cease or at least ease up. Jamie helped her down and she shook the rain from her cloak as he did.

Gazing into the rain, she realized they were still on MacLerie lands, out in the western grazing lands used for their cattle. That meant...

"There," she said, pointing up on the side of the mountain to the west of them. "A shieling."

It was a crude hut, turf-roofed with a low foundation of stones, but it would keep them out of the worst of it. Because of the way it was built into the side of the mountain, it was not easily seen from where they stood. Jamie turned and sought out what she saw. He smiled and nodded.

"Just what we need for shelter from this storm."

They decided it would be quicker to walk and guide the horse along the narrow path on the mountainside than to ride, so Elizabeth pulled her cloak over her head and around her to keep as much rain off as possible. By the time they reached the hut, she was drenched. Jamie led the horse to the side where the trees formed a shelter while she opened the door to the shieling. Elizabeth had to lean into it, for it was stuck from the elements and the age of it. She'd just pushed it open when Jamie joined her, bringing their bags and supplies with him.

Elizabeth ducked her head to enter through the low opening. The hut was small but clean. Though the drovers had long since taken the cattle to the markets in the south, the shieling was left stocked with some meager supplies—a jar of oats, another of flour and one of honey, a griddle pan, some battered metal cups, and some woolen blankets folded on a shelf. The MacLerie steward kept these shelters stocked and clean, and many times these places had saved lives when surprise winter storms moved through the mountains and caught his people outside.

A good thing for them right at this moment.

A quick glance showed the inside was dry, too, with only a small leak in one, easily avoidable corner of the shieling. Other than two low stools, it was empty of furnishings. She moved out of the way so Jamie could enter.

"Not our usual accommodations, but it will keep us dry for now," he said, putting the bags down. "Here, let me have your cloak."

She unfastened it and he lifted the sodden garment from her shoulders. Looking down at the rest of her, she wondered if he was shocked by the trews she wore. Her brother was much taller and larger than she, so she'd been forced to roll them up at the waist to pull the extra fabric into place. It had been years since she and Ciara had worn the scandalous trews, while running through the forests at play. Sliding her hands down onto her thighs, she realized they were soaked through as well. She shivered as the cold, wet fabric plastered itself to her skin.

Jamie had busied himself starting a fire in the small metal brazier after hanging her cloak and his on pegs next to the door. Proving himself quite self-sufficient for a nobleman, he then brought in some chopped blocks of peat to add to it. It would be smoky but would warm them and help dry their cloaks. Soon, the heat of the fire began to fill the hut.

"That should help," he said, facing her. He frowned and shook his head. "You should change out of those wet clothes. I brought your bag in."

He reached for her bag and discovered exactly what she knew would be true—the heavy fabric bag had absorbed as much water as the rest of her had and the gowns inside were wet. When he discovered their condition, he shrugged.

"Well, that is not a choice now, is it?" He pulled one of the blankets from the shelf and shook it out. "At least this will keep you warm while your garments dry."

Now, shivers of another kind shot through her, as she considered undressing with him so close and watching.

She knew it would come to that, once they married, or even before while yet on this journey, but was that to be now? Being as bold as she could, she reached out to take the blanket from him.

# FOUR

James watched as the uncertainty in her gaze changed and she reached out for the blanket he offered. He understood she'd only just comprehended that they were truly alone and truly well into this brave or foolhardy adventure. And accepted the way that it would end—with their marriage and her being bedded, well-bedded, before returning to their families. A lovely blush crept up into her fair-skinned cheeks and her mouth opened slightly as he smiled at her.

Only by taking vows and consummating them would she be protected by the claim of marriage. And whether the vows or the consummation would happen first was not something he'd thought much on...until now!

"Are you worried, Elizabeth? About what will happen between us?" he asked quietly.

Only the sound of the rain outside echoed around them. He had not considered that she would be afraid, not after her bold acceptance of his proposal and their elopement last night. But, her reputation would be ruined if his offer was not honorable. Did she know worry on that?

She let out of breath and sighed. Shaking her head, she turned her back to him and began untying the belt that held the trews up. He snatched up the blanket and held it around her, so she would not be chilled...or embarrassed. Though, truth be told, he wanted to see her naked. Naked and beneath him. Naked, covered only by the length of her brown hair.

James shook himself free of such thoughts, since there would be time enough for all of that, and turned his head away, staring instead at the door. He was not some untried youth who needed to pounce on the woman he wanted, especially since she would be his wife soon enough. And as his wife, they would have a long life ahead of them. So, how they started was an important step and one he would not stumble upon taking.

"Are you hungry?" he asked, as he avoided peeking over the curtain he formed with the blanket.

"A bit," she said, taking the edges of the woolen covering and wrapping it around her shoulders. "I have some food in my bag as well. My mother made meat pies and there were several left. If you look in the bottom of the bag, they are wrapped."

Searching for the meat pies kept him from staring at the lovely, enticing bare shoulders. Or the way she gathered up her wet garments and hung them from various places around the hut. Or the scent of her now-loosened hair as she eased past him and crouched closer to the heat of the peat fire. His hands fisted and relaxed as he reminded himself that he could control the growing desire for her. When the edge of the blanket slipped from her grasp and exposed the slope of her breasts, he sucked in a harsh breath through his clenched teeth.

Turning back his attention to finding the food, he found the pies and removed them, along with some other foodstuffs, and placed them on the shelf. He retrieved the supplies he'd pilfered from the MacLerie kitchen and added them, so they could see what they had and plan how and what they would need.

It would take them no more than one full day of riding to reach the split in the road and the village just beyond it. The priest Lady MacLerie spoke of lived just outside that village, serving the people in the area as a priest in the Old Church. But, until the rains eased and the dirt paths dried out, travel would be nigh to impossible. If they waited out the storms here, at least they would be dry.

"Are you not wet, too?" Her soft voice broke into his moment of inattention.

He stopped himself from tearing loose his own trews and taking his shirt off. But only just, before facing her.

A mischievous smile curled the edges of her mouth and her eyes, eyes that were a deeper shade of blue than his own, twinkled. He tried to understand her expression— was this an invitation?

"A bit. But hungrier than wet," he said, lifting one of the meat pies from the shelf and, having a care for any sauce that might drip from it, breaking it into two pieces. He offered her one and she approached him to get it. "As you must be?"

Her reply came in the form of action—she took the smaller half and bit into it, lapping the sauce from her lower lip before chewing. James watched her, fascinated by everything she did. If being tired, wet and hungry had not vanquished her good spirits, he wondered what would.

"Here, sit closer to the heat. You will never dry if you do not." He pulled one of the stools nearer to the fire and stepped aside.

And he found himself praying both that the blanket around her would slip again and that it would stay in place. Elizabeth grasped the edges firmly as she sat down, arranging the heavy woven fabric around her. She finished the pie as he did, in only a few bites.

"Your mother is a good cook. I hope you have her skills."

"I've learned at her side for years, though I would not suggest you try any bread that I bake," she said, laughing softly. "That has long been my failure." He eased himself down on the other stool, interested in learning more about this side of her.

"What is your favorite thing to make then? Pies like these? Or something sweet?" He had a weakness for the cakes and treats his family's cook made. She blushed then and glanced away before trying to answer him. Now, he was even more curious!

"My father says that I make the best...heather ale of all the brewers in the Lairig Dubh."

He leaned his head back and laughed. Not once had she mentioned such a thing during the times they'd talked. And he'd heard no inkling of her talent, but then he'd been betrothed to Ciara and most of the talk centered on her and her extensive—and rather formidable—skills and talents. Not on her shadow, Elizabeth, who'd grown up in the village and whose parents served the laird.

"And did your mother teach you that as well?" Though these Highlanders were known more for their *uisge beatha*, ale was the favored drink of the Lowlands and the lands that had belonged, and some that did still, to the Norse in the north.

"Nay," she said. "My mother is known for her cooking, but her sister is known for her ale." She laughed then, the sound of it warming his heart. "Now that she is widowed, the earl has offered to buy a place for her in the burgh of Glasgow or in Aberdeen to set up her own business. They would be partners."

"'Tis a good thing to know, Elizabeth. At least my wife might have employment." She watched him with widened eyes then, as though divining his meaning.

"Is that what you think will happen after—" she waved her hand between them "—this?" When he hesitated, she slid down to her knees, bringing her with reach before him. "Please, I pray you, tell me."

He placed his hands on her shoulders and rubbed her arms, gently easing up and down in an effort to offer comfort after he'd upset her. Insulting a man like Connor and breaking faith with him was more dangerous than he wanted to dwell upon. With the earl's allies and connections across the kingdom and beyond, the Murray name would be deemed dishonored by his actions now— if the MacLerie wished it so.

"I do not know what to expect. Although I spoke with the MacLerie, I do not expect him to be happy with the choice I made. But you are his kin and I don't think he will take action against you." That was why James's note spoke of his abduction of Elizabeth rather than making it seem that she was a willing partner in this. It might protect her from Connor's wrath.

"What would he do to you?" she whispered, her gaze filled with worry. Though he would rather not think on these matters now, they must discuss it.

"I understood when I asked you to marry me that it would violate the contracts negotiated by my father. Not just the marriage contract, but trade arrangements as well.

And the MacLerie does not like to be defied," he said. She nodded, knowing the earl better than he did and knowing the truth of the rumors and tales of his harsh actions and past sins. "I think it just depends on how angry my father is and how much damage the earl wants to inflict."

She paled then, losing the color in her cheeks until he thought she might faint. Drawing her closer, he held her against him. "Once our marriage is a fact he cannot argue with, we will return and face him. Face my father also. But, first I think we should let the anger cool."

"Better to face them with the deed done then?" she asked, lifting her face until it was but a scant inch from his own. Deed done? Aye, he wanted a certain deed to be done at this moment!

"Aye. Better to beg forgiveness than to ask permission, I think," he said, surprised at how rough his voice sounded as he spoke. Thick. It was thick with the rising desire he felt for her.

He could resist no more. Her rosy lips, parted slightly in invitation, called to him. James gave in, taking her mouth with his even as he grabbed the blanket she wore around her to hold her where he wanted her. If they would be together, he wanted it to begin now. Now, before anything or anyone came between them.

"Elizabeth, be mine? Now?" he whispered against her lips.

She answered without words. He felt her hands release the blanket and creep up around his neck to embrace him. As her bare skin touched his wet clothing, she shivered even as the heat of her mouth burned his.

"Here, let me," he said, drawing back a few inches.

He tugged the wet shirt off—as he'd wanted to do before—and then loosened his belt and pushed his trews down, kicking them aside. James took hold of the blanket's edges once more and brought Elizabeth back to him. He watched her face for any sign of fear or dismay or hesitation and saw none. But for a quick glance down as he faced her, she met his gaze and then accepted his embrace.

His cock rose against his groin and the softness of her bare skin against it simply made him want her more. Her tightened nipples pressed against his chest, and his blood caught fire and raced through his veins.

Elizabeth did not want to breathe. She did not want to see. She simply wanted to feel, to feel all the sensations as Jamie claimed her body as he had her heart. Only nervous about his reaction to her impure condition, she did not hesitate when he tugged her to him. Leaning against the hard ridge of flesh that showed he desired her, she rubbed her belly against him.

And felt his reaction.

Her breasts lay heavy against his muscular chest, the sprinkling of curly hair that was shades darker than the pale brown hair on his head, teasing the now-sensitive tips and making her gasp with each movement. An aching heat began to throb in the center of her.

Was it sinful, as her mother had said, to want to lay with him? To be his even before their vows were spoken? He had taken such risks to marry her—alienating his family, angering one of the most powerful and most dangerous men in the kingdom, risking everything to be with her. Her indecision lasted a brief moment as she understood that he was worth risking what she could give him—her heart, her body, her love and her support as his wife.

She slid her fingers into his hair, entangling them as he moved his hands over her skin, caressing her until she reached up and offered her mouth to him. He teased her skin and her mouth with light, feathery touches until she wanted to scream out in pleasure and frustration. He laughed then and met her gaze for a moment before tilting his head and taking her mouth...and her very breath!

Now, his fingers kneaded the muscles of her back as he used his tongue to taste her mouth deeply. Then, his strong hands grasped her buttocks and pulled her up and against his erection. When her legs spread open to encircle his hips, she moaned as the hard flesh rubbed against that heated, aching place. Without clothing between them, this was almost too pleasurable to bear. Elizabeth clenched her knees tightly to hold him close and then arched against him.

His reaction was swift. Jamie lifted his mouth from hers and trailed kisses—hungry, ravenous kisses—down her neck. Lifting her higher, he used his teeth against her breasts until he took one of her nipples fully into his mouth. Her body arched without thought, as though there was a string being pulled through her with each touch. His teeth teased the tip until she did scream out. His caress turned into a gentle suckling, but her body was like a wild thing of its own against him. His hands moved but did not release her and she could do nothing but enjoy his attentions.

With her hands tangled in his hair, she did not know if she held him in place or urged him on. She did not care. When his mouth took the other breast and his tongue relentlessly laved its tip, her head dropped back and she panted as everything within her tightened to an almost-unbearable tension. She sought the release she knew waited for her by rubbing harder and faster against him, but it remained just out of her reach.

Finally, Jamie held her as he knelt down on the blanket she now realized he'd tossed aside some time before. With his body pressing hers to the floor of the croft, she waited for him to seek his release within her. Only by clenching her teeth together did she prevent the begging words from being keened out to him. It would take little action on his part to lift himself and plunge within her, and she urged him to do so with her hips and that hot, wet place between her legs.

He laughed then, a deep-throated sound that came out hoarse with passion and lust. It was time. It was time. It had to be...

She almost yelled at him when he eased to his side, but the touch of his hand between her legs made it impossible to speak. He stared at her, watching her as he pressed down with the heel of his hand and slipped a finger into her. It both eased the tension and spurred it on and made it worse. The second finger moved along with the first and she dropped her knees open so he could touch her more fully.

"Elizabeth," he whispered, as those two fingers became implements of a sensuous torture. "Open for me, lass," he urged. When he kissed her breasts and began to suckle one and then the other, in a pace matching his fingers, she knew she would fall apart soon.

Jamie moved his hand and used his thumb, finding at last that small nub that ached the most. One flick was all it took to send her screaming into release. But he did not stop, he stroked her over and over as her muscles tightened throughout her body and then everything broke free within her. Pleasure and heat flowed deep inside of her as she spasmed in time with his caresses. Her mind wandered as her body shivered and shook.

Elizabeth had barely come back to herself when Jamie lifted himself between her legs. Even as pleasure yet pulsed through her, she knew it would happen again when he filled her. Reaching down to touch his flesh, she held her breath as he began to lower his body to hers.

A flash of lightning filled the shieling, followed by a loud ominous crash of thunder and what sounded like an explosion outside. Jamie turned toward the terrible sound as he quickly climbed to his feet. Grabbing the blanket around her, Elizabeth tried to follow, but her legs shook and would not support her. She sank back to the floor, her body still in the throes of passion, to wait for Jamie to return.

# FIVE

By the time he reached and opened the door, he could only watch as the spooked horse charged off down the hill toward the thicker woods to the south. Walking around to the back of the shieling, James discovered a huge branch of a tree on the ground near where the horse had been, smoke curling up from where the lighting had struck. Only the heavy, soaking rains and the wet turf that served as a roof prevented the entire hut from burning to the ground. Running his hands through his hair, he stared at the damage and then looked to where the horse had last been seen.

The icy cold rain pelting his naked skin brought him to his senses. He was standing out in the rain with not a stitch of clothing on. The torrents of rain had not lessened and the bite of their sharp pellets stung him in places he did not wish to have damaged. Especially not with the lovely and equally naked Elizabeth waiting inside for him. First he found a bucket and filled it from the trough. Pouring it on the tree where it yet burned, he watched until the last embers died out. Dumping another bucketful to be sure, he turned and searched down the hillside for any sign of the terrified creature.

Sweet Christ, he needed to find that horse!

It would take days for them to walk to the village during which time the earl's men would surely catch up with them. He did not have enough coin to purchase another one and still buy the supplies they would need in order to stay safely away from his family and hers until the worst was past. Looking up at the relentless rain pouring from the black and dangerous sky and then down at his condition, he shook his head.

He needed to find that horse.

Walking back to the door, he could not stop himself from cringing as another crash of lightning reminded him of the present danger of the storm. He knocked first, for a reason he could not fathom, before opening the door and entering. He'd left her naked as tremors of passion flowed through her and did not know what to expect now.

Elizabeth sat cross-legged on the floor, almost where he'd left her. She'd drawn the blanket up around her and only the tip of her soft boots peeked through under the edge of the covering. He made no attempts to cover himself and he felt his cock harden once more as she watched him walk from the door to where she sat.

Her hair was tousled and her mouth well-kissed. She'd melted beneath his touch and his mouth and made the most incredible sounds as he caressed her most private places. An exciting blend of passion and innocence, she had given herself over to him in a way he'd never expected. In a way he prayed would be the normal way of things between them. Once they were married and she was his without question and without challenge.

If only...

The sound of another crash of thunder brought him back on task.

"The horse was spooked by the lightning and bolted. I have to go find it," he said, grabbing his damp garments from where he'd tossed them. Fighting the fabric's resistance, he managed to get dressed and pull his boots back on. "I cannot let it wander too far in this storm."

"Should I come with you?" she asked, glancing over his shoulder to the open door and the storm outside.

"Nay," he said. "Why should you get wet again? I will search for it and bring it back." He leaned over and touched her cheek with the back of his hand. She rested against it, closing her eyes as she did. He noticed the dark smudges under her eyes then and realized she was exhausted. "Rest while I'm gone. We have a long journey ahead of us when the rains stop. Now though, I must find that damned, cowardly horse."

James turned and left before he could finish ravishing her as his body was urging him to do now. He followed the path down the hillside, sliding in the mud more times than he would like to admit. The rain did not ease at all as he spent the rest of the morning and part of the afternoon searching. It took hours but he did track it down, catch it and lead it back to the shieling on the hill. By that time, the rains had changed from torrential to heavy downpours and the lightning had eased and no longer crashed all about them.

As he walked back, trying not to wear any more of the road and mud than he already was, it struck him that he had been more adventurous and daring in the last day and night than in all his life before. And other than the horse's escape, which could be squarely blamed on the storm, he'd gotten along well in his plan. Facing the consequences would be the difficult part but he would do so gladly with Elizabeth at his side.

He had lived his life by following the rules and being the son his parents expected and needed him to be. Only meeting Elizabeth and realizing what his life would like without her spurred him to leave practicality and pragmatism behind and seek the life he wanted. Even after the ludicrous morning escapade of chasing a horse through the forest, James believed everything would work out after all.

There were no burning trees upon his return and the shieling looked the same as when he'd left it. Leading the horse up the steep hillside, he tied it, more securely this time, behind the dwelling and eased the door open.

She lay on her side, with a hand tucked under her cheek, sleeping. The fire had warmed the hut nicely and he closed the door so the heat did not escape. Stripping out of his dripping clothes, he took another blanket and wrapped it around himself. Slowly so as to not wake her, James lay down next to her and gathered her closer in his arms. As she always seemed to do, Elizabeth accepted his embrace and moved closer to him.

The rain came down in a steady pace outside and James hoped that meant an end was close. These Highlands were much wetter than his home in Perthshire. He would not miss the constant dampness and dreariness when they returned south. He would take her to the coast, to see the sea and walk on the sandy beaches there.

His thoughts drifted and soon, the warmth of her body and the hypnotic sound of the rain eased his way into sleep.

Elizabeth knew the moment he returned but she feigned sleep. Unsure of how to face him after the way she'd behaved, she preferred to let some time pass before facing him. Watching him undress through half-closed eyes, she admired his body once more.

All of it.

Though not as brawny as some of her MacLerie kin, his body was muscular and lean. She'd watched him ride and fight, even taking on Tavis MacLerie and holding his own against the consummate MacLerie warrior. She'd felt every inch of him when he held her close, both during their...activities of a pleasurable nature and then in the comfortable grasp of sleep. Unlike Ciara, who yearned for more and for different than him, Jamie Murray was perfect for her.

She'd found one of her gowns was dry and dressed in it. After seeing to her needs and while waiting for water to boil in the pot for tea she would make, she watched him sleep.

If only she'd been perfect for him.

She sighed, leaning her cheek against her hand, worried now over what was to come between them. Elizabeth had no idea two years ago of how one error in judgment, one lapse in control, could affect her future happiness. But now, as she would face the true repercussions of her shameful behavior, she wondered how Jamie would react when he discovered that another man had been her first lover.

Would he cast her aside? Would he expose her to public shame when he discovered she had lain with another man? Would he overlook such a failing in the woman who would bear his children and his name?

Marriage to take care of the mistake had not been an option—so the earl had taken care of the matter between her and a visitor, there to negotiate a treaty, quietly. The man, a nobleman high in standing and wealth and with powerful friends and family at court, had claimed he thought her available for bed-sport. She'd been a stupid, naive and inexperienced young woman who thought he spoke the truth about his feelings for her, never realizing it was all part of his game to bed whatever woman he could.

Once she confirmed that she was not with child, Connor had handled the situation as efficiently as he handled most things in his life. The man involved was never welcomed in Lairig Dubh again, indeed, never welcomed by any of the MacLerie allies or friends or branches of the clan.

Though certain very few knew the true reason, Elizabeth knew exactly how Connor MacLerie worked—a touch of genuine concern for his kin mixed with ruthless determination to make things the way he wanted them to be. She'd witnessed it many times as she grew up and knew of even more times through Ciara, as her friend worked at Duncan MacLerie's side as peacemaker and negotiator for the earl's business interests. Connor got what he wanted and made whatever he wanted to happen happen, and rarely was he thwarted.

Elizabeth swallowed deeply as she realized she and Jamie had done exactly that. And the price that they would pay for their defiance was yet to be known. She reached down and dropped some of the crushed betony into the pot, enjoying the aroma of the herb. A cup of hot tea would feel good right now.

She wrapped the edge of her skirt around her skirt and lifted the steaming pot from the fire. Carrying it over to the table near the shelves, she poured two cups. A drop or two of honey would make it the way she liked it. When she finished, she turned to find Jamie watching her.

"I think I like this," he said, as he lifted his arms out from under the blanket and stretched. Leaning up on his elbows, he accepted the cup she offered him. "It will be no hardship having you as my wife."

"You haven't tasted my cooking yet, so do not rush to judgment," she teased. He sat up, sipping the steaming tea with a care, and nodded to her.

"Well, I have yet to experience that, but this is wonderful. What is in it?"

"Betony from the lady's garden. A drop of honey."

"'Tis good. I like it. My thanks for making it."

He stood then, holding the blanket around his hips and holding his cup out to her. She took it, her mouth dry in spite of a mouthful of tea. That tea sat on her tongue and refused to be swallowed. Jamie reached for his trews with his free hand, testing their dryness.

"How long have I slept?" he asked as he dropped the blanket and pulled the trousers on.

She would have answered if she was able to, but the sight of him, even from the back, took her breath away. Worse, her hand lifted to touch him before she realized it. To glide her hands over the strong muscles of his back, to let them drop down over his sculpted buttocks and to touch the hard muscles in his thighs... Lost for a moment in desire, she forgot he'd asked her a question. When he turned and met her gaze, the corner of his mouth lifted in a smile that told her he knew exactly what she was thinking. Elizabeth let her hand drop and tried to think about what he'd asked.

"How long...?" he prompted.

"'Tis past sunset now," she replied. "You were exhausted so I did not wake you."

She watched as he found his shirt and pulled it over his head. Now, she wanted to run her fingers through his hair, smoothing the tangles and feeling its texture. Pulling her thoughts away from his body, she cleared her throat.

"Since it was still raining, I did not think you planned to leave yet." Elizabeth gave him his cup when he reached for it. He shook his head.

"Traveling the muddy path would be dangerous in the dark. By morning, hopefully the rains will cease and the roads will dry out." He stepped past her and looked at their store of food on the shelf. "Are you hungry?"

Her stomach chose that moment to let him know exactly how hungry she was, grumbling loudly enough to be heard by both of them. She covered it with her hands, but it was too late. Her mother always said she a healthy appetite and she would admit to loving a good meal. "I suppose I am."

Jamie laughed then, taking the two remaining pies from their cloth wrappers and placing them on the table. He moved the stools next to the table and waited for her to sit. She filled their cups with the remaining tea and sat. They ate their plain meal in companionable silence.

"The unavoidable will happen," Jamie said as she cleaned up the crumbs from their food. She stopped in motion and stared at him, thinking he meant to bed her now. "You will have to cook for me in the morn." He laughed then and nodded. "With your mother's pies done and needing some of the leftover food for our journey on the morrow, you must make us some of those oatcakes I keep hearing about."

She forgot that he was a Lowlander by birth and that, other than this and two other journeys north, he spent little time away from the area of his birth. The language that they now spoke should have reminded her, but she could slip in and out of Scots easily. He spoke little of her Gàidhlig and struggled with it.

"Every Highland boy and girl is taught to make oatcakes," she said, smiling at him. "I can teach you how to, if you would like?"

"Is that so I cannot blame you if they burn or are too dry?" he teased.

"Aye," she admitted. "I mean, nay! I have mastered the simple oatcake, sir. 'Tis the more involved baked foods that escape my abilities."

"Very well," he said, gazing at her with a new

intensity in his blue eyes. "If you promise to teach me how to make an oatcake in the morn, I will teach you something this night."

Her body reacted before she even realized the sensual promise in his words, heat spilling through her belly and into her breasts. The deep tones of his voice made her want to peel off her gown and melt at his feet.

She should be ashamed at the way she reacted, without thinking first of her unmarried state, but she knew he was an honorable man and he would stand by his promises to her. Well, she prayed he would when he discovered her secret.

But, really, all the time she spent examining her conscience seemed to matter little, or not at all, when he lifted his hand and traced the outline of her mouth with his finger. And it mattered less when that same finger slid down and touched her breast, drawing a circle around the sensitive tip before rubbing it with his thumb. Her body ached and arched toward him. Before he could touch her any other place, she covered his hand with hers and asked the question she wanted to.

"What will you teach me, Jamie?"

# SIX

What would he teach her?

She already loved him. She already wanted him. She'd pledged herself and her life to him. And she made him burn hotter than any fire.

What could he teach her?

James stepped closer and touched only his mouth to hers, leaving a few inches between them. Lifting his mouth while staying so close he could feel her breath against his lips, he revealed some of what he wanted to show her this night...and every night of their lives together.

"I want to teach you how good it can be between us." He kissed the edge of her chin and trailed a path of kisses along the line of her jaw until he reached her ear.

"I will teach you to find the way you like to be

touched," he whispered into her ear. He traced the curves of her ear with his tongue, finally gaining the sigh he wanted to hear. James felt her body tremble and move an infinitesimal amount toward him. He wanted her panting and hot and ready for him and he knew from this morning how to make her so. Her breasts were very sensitive to his kisses and caresses.

"I will teach you how to seek and gain pleasure." Now he moved to stand behind her, easing the length of her hair to one side and biting the cord between her neck and shoulder gently. The gown she wore was no barrier to what he did, for she did shudder then. His own body reacted now, his flesh ready to join with her. Now.

James unlaced the back of her gown, kissing his way down her spine as he slid the garment off her shoulders, allowing it to fall to her hips. After pulling his shirt off, he touched her from behind, moving his hands along the bottom of her ribs, around until they rested just below her breasts. She leaned against him then, sending shocks into his body. Her hot, smooth skin against his inflamed his desire for her even more.

But, he would control the need that simmered within him and make their first time memorable...and immensely pleasurable for her. James kissed her exposed neck as he cupped her breasts in his hands, pulling her back so that she could feel how much he desired her. She gasped over and over as he rubbed his thumbs across her nipples until they tightened.

"Jamie," she whispered on a sigh. "You undo me."

He smiled then, knowing what more was still to happen between them. He had only just begun his seduction of her. When he covered her breasts and massaged them, then teased the tips again, she rolled her head against his shoulder and moaned aloud.

Now, he traced the lovely mounds before moving lower, onto her stomach then lower still, pushing the gown until it slid the rest of the way to the floor. Naked but for her stockings and low boots, she arched against his hands, while pressing her beautiful arse against him. He closed his eyes and imagined her bent over as he plumbed her feminine depths from behind. He thrust then, losing control for only a moment, but she felt his hardness and rubbed that arse against it harder.

He placed his hands on her hips and moved against her. She gifted him with another delicious moan, but the sound he wanted to hear came when he crept his fingers down across her belly and touched the curls covering her mons. Her mouth dropped open and she began to pant. James smiled and moved his fingers lower until he felt the wetness there between her legs. Using both hands, he caressed her there until he felt her allow her body to relax on his. Then he rubbed harder and faster and deeper until he found that tiny bud buried within that would make her scream.

"And I will teach you to scream," he said as he increased the pressure and pace against that part of her that would give her both pleasure and then release. "Scream for me, my love."

She did then and his body thrust at her from behind, his erection aching and so ready to take that final step. The lovely, lustful sound of her voice, raised and rough, as her release did happen, almost unmanned him. He nearly lost his grip on her, but he held on and continued to push her body on and on until he'd wrought a full measure of release from her.

He thought she would melt limply against him, so her next action surprised him. She reached up and drew his head down, taking his mouth in a kiss so deep and so hot that it left him breathless. She turned in his embrace and now held onto him. James scooped her up in his arms, their mouths yet touching, their tongues still tasting and stroking deeply, and laid her on the blankets spread there.

Elizabeth reached up and unbuckled his belt, loosening his trews and pushing them down. His cock was freed, and she leaned back and watched him. James moved to kneel between her legs and she shifted to allow him there. He bent over and kissed her, using his hands to make her ready for him. When her hips lifted to meet his caresses, he knew she was.

"Elizabeth. My love," he whispered as he held onto her hips and brought them up off the blanket. "I will have a care for you in this, lass," he promised.

The touch of her hand on his and the expression in her gaze surprised him. Not exactly dread, but clearly she was not as fearless as she'd been only moments before. Then, it was gone and she laid her head back and closed her eyes.

It was time to claim her and make her truly his.

Finally.

He leaned down and began to enter her, slowly but without hesitation. He'd not bedded many virgins, only one before her, and the tightness did not surprise him. Her flesh fit around his as he moved deeper within her. James did not pause until he was completely buried inside her. Only as he began to move, sliding out a little then thrusting back in, did he realize that there had been nothing to resist or slow his entry.

But, when she lifted her legs around his hips, bringing him deeper still, he lost the ability to think about anything but making her scream once more. Plunging harder and faster as she urged him on, he felt her body tighten. His release was close. Too close. Reaching between their bodies, he found that sensitive bud and caressed it until her release began. James filled her and eased out, filled her and eased out, over and over until she shuddered and tightened around his cock.

He did not stop until she collapsed, panting and sweating beneath him. His seed exploded from him, dowsing her womb and making him grunt with satisfaction. Only when the last spasm emptied him did he stop, holding himself on his elbows so she could breathe. Then, still within her, James rolled them to their sides and he waited for the exquisite pleasure to ebb before pulling his flesh from hers.

Lying together, neither one spoke. He pushed her hair from her face and kissed her forehead. Instead of meeting his gaze, she tucked her head under his chin in silence. He caressed her, rubbing her back and holding her close as he tried to come up with the words to say.

For what did a man say to his beloved, the woman who would be his wife, when he now knew he had not been the first inside her.

Elizabeth had not been a virgin when he'd claimed her.

Young Dougal paced the yard outside Broch Dubh keep, waiting for some order from the earl. Surely Connor MacLerie would not allow this insult, this kidnapping, to go unanswered. No matter that it had ended well for his friend Tavis and for Ciara—they were married now, only hours ago, as everyone in the clan had always thought they would.

But, the Murrays' heir had stolen another MacLerie, forcing her, according to the note he'd left, to leave with him. Elizabeth MacLerie would be ruined if James Murray did not take her as wife. Surely Connor would take action against him for this flagrant disrespect?

As Tavis's second-in-command, young Dougal knew it would fall to him to carry out whatever orders the earl gave and he was ready, armed and packed to leave as soon as Connor gave word. Now, hours after James's actions were uncovered and hours after Ciara and Tavis had married, no word had come. He had not been called by the earl.

When the summons came, it was well after dark and he strode through the keep to the earl's chambers in the tower. Climbing the stairs, he was not surprised to find the lady also present. If it were unseemly for a woman to know a man's business, the earl cared not. For as long as Dougal could remember, the lady was always at his side, giving counsel and sharing her opinions as was her wont to do.

Duncan, the man the earl relied on to negotiate the clan's treaties, stood in the corner and Rurik, the commander of all MacLerie warriors, was there at his side. Both nodded as he entered but said nothing. Dougal walked to the earl and the lady and bowed, awaiting his orders.

"Dougal, you know that James Murray took Elizabeth?" Connor said. Dougal grimaced, but nodded. "I want you to select two other men and track them down. My best guess..." The earl glanced at his wife before continuing. He looked over and noticed the embarrassed blush spread across her face before turning back to the earl. "My best guess is that he heads to the village near the Glasgow road south. There is a priest of the old faith there."

Dougal clenched his jaw and ground his teeth at this news. He must act on the earl's orders and do nothing more or less than he said. No matter that Elizabeth was his younger sister and he wanted to rip this man apart, limb by limb, piece by piece, and make him suffer for kidnapping her. He took a deep breath and released it, holding onto his fury and planning to deal with it when he could.

"I know the place. We passed it on our journey here from Perthshire." Already calculating the distance and time it would take to reach the village, Dougal realized they could reach it in a matter of hours if they pushed. Sooner if they used the mountain pass south.

"I want them returned here," Connor said, his face giving away nothing of how he felt about the actions of this man. "I want him alive."

"If he has harmed her or forced her, I will..." Dougal began, clenching his hands into fists.

"I want him returned alive, Dougal. Tavis assured me that you were ready to lead in his stead. If he was wrong and you cannot manage this task, I will get someone else."

He need only return James Murray alive, the earl did not say he could not mete out some punishment—which was his right as Elizabeth's brother. Piece by piece could wait until after the earl had levied his judgment on the man.

"I understand, my lord," he said, nodding in acceptance of the limitations placed on him. "Do you wish me to leave now or at first light?"

Connor began to speak, but stopped when the lady touched his arm. They exchanged only a glance, no words, but some understanding was reached in that silent conversation.

"Now," he said.

"Connor!" the lady said sharply. Dougal grimaced, waiting for the earl's reprimand but all he heard was the soft laughter of the two men watching the exchange.

"Jocelyn, if he was true to his words, the deed is done and there will be no turning back from it. If he dawdled or delayed, I would have him returned here and deal with his lack of honor sooner rather than later. When things cannot be undone."

The earl never raised his voice, yet Dougal cringed at the tone. The lady? She did not seem to understand her peril and continued to argue. Dougal forced his body still and fought the urge to take several steps back.

"Connor, I pray thee, do not..."

The earl stood so quickly that Dougal never even saw him move. Connor stood so that he blocked Jocelyn from everyone else in the room and no one could hear their harshly whispered words. A few very awkward minutes passed as they conversed, argued really, and then the earl sat back down. The lady wore a dark scowl on her face that matched his—clearly neither were pleased with how things were going.

"You can choose the men and leave this night."

The words echoed in the chamber and Dougal waited

for the lady to speak in protest. Silence filled the room, though from the mutinous expression on her face, the lady would not be silent for long after he left.

"Very well, my lord," Dougal answered with a bow, offering a nod to the lady and to Duncan and Rurik, who followed him out.

He reached the bottom of the stairway, thinking about which men he should choose. This was his first command situation and his choice would reflect on him. Since it involved his sister and her reputation, he wanted men who could be discreet. And since he planned to bring James Murray back alive but not untouched, he wanted men who could be trusted.

Niall and Shaw.

"Dougal, wait a moment," Duncan called out to him before he left the tower. "I would have a word with you."

Dougal stopped until the two reached him. They were both among the most experienced and most loyal of all the earl's men and their advice would be valuable.

"Do not let your personal feelings get in the way of your duty," Rurik advised. "No matter that your sister is involved."

Dougal nodded at the commander's words, though in truth he would find it difficult not to remember his sister's part in this.

"Do not let your temper loose," Duncan advised. "Though Connor said only 'alive,' he would be furious if James Murray comes back too badly damaged." So, the counselor had heard exactly what Dougal had. "Mistakes are made when a man's blood is running hot, whether caused by lust or insult. Do not make a mistake in how you treat the Murrays' heir."

Good advice, even though Dougal had already planned how the man would suffer for having shamed his sister. He would be alive on his return—beaten, battered and abused, but alive. He nodded at the two and took his leave. Why the earl had waited this long before sending him, he knew not. Dougal only knew that he would find them and prevent his sister from making the biggest mistake of her life.

Within a few hours, the three of them were on their way south and west to track down his sister and the man who would dishonor her.

# SEVEN

Elizabeth lay wrapped in his arms, fighting back the tears that had threatened for hours. Ever since...

Ever since the most wonderful experience of her life.

Now she waited for the rebuke and repudiation to come. If she was a coward for lying here in silence, savoring these last few moments in his embrace before the inevitable ending, so be it.

The first bit of sunlight found her still awake and wondering what Jamie would do and what he would say. She'd promised to teach him to make oatcakes, but would he even care about that this morn? No longer content to wait about, she slipped free of him and gathered her clothes and dressed. She smiled as she realized she'd slept, and been tupped, in her stockings and low boots.

She found his muddied clothes from his pursuit of the wayward horse and took them outside, brushing the worst of the dried, caked dirt from them. Turning them inside out and rolling them up, Elizabeth planned to wash them when they found a good place to do so. Then, she went back inside to do the thing she'd promised him she would do before everything between them had changed.

Within a few minutes, she was mixing together some of the oats, a bit of salt she'd found, a small amount of honey and some water. She had no butter to add, but these plain oatcakes would fill their bellies. After adding some peat to the low fire, she put the heavy griddle pan on to heat it. Stepping quietly so as not to wake him, she only realized Jamie was awake when he reached out and grabbed her gown as she passed by him.

"I have the oatcakes ready to cook," she said, trying for a brighter tone than what she felt. And purposely avoiding any talk about what had happened between them.

He sat up then, pushing the blankets aside as he stood and stretched. And damn her eyes! Elizabeth watched every move he made in case this was the last time she would see him so. If he noticed he said nothing as he walked outside to see to his needs and to check on the horse...and the weather. By the time he returned, the first batch of cakes were cooking on the griddle, filling the small dwelling with the delicious aroma of oats baking. He dressed before saying anything to her.

"So what ingredients did you use?" he asked, walking up behind her as she took the first batch off and dropped spoonfuls of new batter on the hot surface. She felt the heat of his body from where he stood looking over her shoulder.

"Oats, salt, honey and water," she said, trying to ignore the longing within her heart to reach out to him and beg him to forgive her for the deception she played on him. Instead, she concentrated on the words she could say. "I would have added some butter if I was at home, but they will turn out without it in a pinch."

"I think this qualifies as a pinch, does it not?" he asked as he stepped away and began to gather up all the clothing they'd removed from their bags.

She noticed he would glance over at her every so often and she waited for him to say something. But he did not. By the time she'd finished cooking the last of the cakes, he'd packed all their belongings and supplies and put them by the door of the shieling. Soon, they would leave and all evidence of what wondrous things had happened between them would be gone.

But not forgotten. Not by her. Not for a very long time.

Not ever.

She set the plate on the table and poured some water into the cups now. He took his place on the other stool and lifted one of the oatcakes to his mouth. She waited, his opinion being important to her after their teasing about her cooking abilities. He bit into it and chewed. Then he took more. She chose one but waited for him to finish his before beginning.

"For a bit of oats, salt, honey and water, these are delicious, Elizabeth," he said. He smiled but did not meet her gaze. "Clearly you can cook oatcakes."

Another deception on her part and one that had been going on for some time. Not even her mother knew of her true cooking abilities for, though skilled in it, she hated it. So, she purposely ruined meals until she was allowed to do the thing she enjoyed more—working with her aunt.

She thought on her aunt's plan and realized it might be a godsend, for when she returned this time in shame, Connor would never let her stay. At least, he might consider sending her along with her aunt, far from Lairig Dubh in one of the cities.

"Jamie," she began before losing any words she planned to say to him. How could she explain?

"You were not a virgin," he said, softly. Neither his tone nor his expression gave away his feelings on the matter. He stated it as the fact it was.

"Nay."

"When?" he asked without meeting her eyes. She understood the significance of his question even if it was asked in a calm voice. Did she carry another man's bairn?

"More than a year ago," she whispered. "Jamie, I..."

Again, unable to defend herself, she let the words drift off into the silence.

She reached out to touch his hand, but he moved it before she could. Did he think she would deny it? She waited for him to speak, but he said nothing while reaching for another of the oatcakes. They continued to eat their fill without speaking, with the only sounds being the water jug or the plate being passed between them.

Elizabeth rose and wrapped the ones left to take with them and used the water to put out the fire. Jamie checked it and once content that it was out, he began to carry the bags outside. By the time she'd cleaned and put away the griddle and water jug and gathered her own bag, he had the horse saddled and the rest of their bags secured.

He pulled the door of the shieling closed and tied the rope to keep wild animals and the like from getting inside. Then he mounted and held out his hand to her to help her up. 'Twas at that time she noticed the thick blanket he'd placed behind his saddle, where she would sit. At first, it confused her, but then the reason became clear—he thought she would be uncomfortable riding this morning.

Truth be told, she was sore, though not as much as she'd been that first time. Not a virgin, however she was not accustomed to tupping and not as vigorously as they had. Now, she felt heat enter her cheeks as she thought of just how vigorous it had been. Coughing to clear her throat, she accepted his hand-up and adjusted the skirts of her gown and shift and the length of her cloak around her legs. Trews were absolutely more convenient for riding, but her family and most of the village would be scandalized if they witnessed it.

Jamie guided the horse down the now-drying path at a slow pace. Though the rains had stopped several hours before, the mud would take longer to dry out completely—if it did before the next storms passed through the area. They made it back to the bottom of the hill and Jamie surprised her by heading south.

"Where are you heading?" she asked over his shoulder. Surely after last night's discovery, he would call things off between them.

"To the village. Where else would we be going?" he said, drawing the horse to a halt. "Nothing has changed, Elizabeth." And yet it had, in so many ways she could not even begin to identify or describe.

"And you still wish to marry me?" she asked. For was that not the primary question to voice?

"I gave you my word when we made our plans to leave Lairig Dubh. I will not go back on that even now."

Was her heart bleeding? The piercing pain caused by his lack of enthusiasm and tone of entrapment took her breath away. Unable to speak, almost unable to remain upright, his truth tore her apart. He would marry her because he'd given his word. In spite of her lack of virginity and deception, he would continue in their bargain because he'd given his word. After breaking it with Ciara, she knew him well enough to know he would not do that again. But, where were the soft words of yesterday? The pledges of love and hope and a life together?

She really had no right to disagree, so she sat behind him holding on to the edge of the saddle to balance and barely touching him, as he guided the horse to the main pathway and they continued on their journey. He was once more trapped in a marriage bargain because he needed to do the right thing by her. But this time, she'd been the cause of it and would not be his escape but his captor.

James heard the pain in her voice and felt it in her body as she sat behind him, stiff as a fence post. Had she thought he would disavow her? Had she thought they would have an ugly, angry confrontation over her lack of virginity? Part of him did want that, that primitive part he buried deep inside and controlled and had planned it when he'd asked the question of her. The part more like these Highland warriors than the Scottish nobleman he was raised to be.

She had given herself to a man before him.

Had she loved that man before him? If so, why was she not married to him? How had he not heard of her disgrace? Or had she managed to keep her fall a secret?

This, he realized, was what came from living for passion and making decisions based on lust and love rather than calm, rational discussions and reasons. He'd broken the code he'd lived by and now he would pay the price for such arrogance and bad judgment.

He shifted and glanced back at her to see how she fared this morn. James had not noticed her moving with any obvious pain or discomfort and she'd given no sign that he'd hurt her when he'd bedded her. Remembering for a moment the sheer pleasure of their joining, he tried to understand why she'd lied to him.

Was her past experience the reason for her enjoyment of the physical pleasure between them?

Now her acceptance of his touches and caresses took on a new meaning. Did she compare him to whomever she had in her bed before him? Did she regret what they had done? She'd never paused or shown any reticence in the act or anything he'd done. Would she be so at ease in bed if she'd been forced in the past? Was that how she lost her virtue?

That would explain some of his confusion, for why would Ciara remain friends with a woman who had no honor? Why would Connor allow her to remain in Lairig Dubh if she brought shame on her family? She would have been sent away if this had happened in his family. So, why did Connor allow her to stay?

If she had told him the truth, told him of her lack of virtue, would he have pledged his love or promised to marry her? Would he have risked everything—family, fortune and future—to be with her? Would he have fallen in love with her? At this moment, he just did not know. And at this very moment, she could be carrying his child which gave him fewer choices.

She sighed then, a soft sound he doubted she even was aware of, but he heard it. His body heard it and he fought to keep the desire he had for her, even now knowing what he did, under control. Until they cleared things up between them—though he was not certain he wanted to learn the details of her past—he would not lie with her. It might be too late to turn back, but it was not too late to try to gain some honesty between them.

The sun broke through the clouds then, promising an easier path this day. Pushing off the doubts and the questions, he took the road's measure and decided they could safely ride faster.

"Hold onto to me, Elizabeth," he said over his shoulder. "We must ride faster to make up some of the distance."

Elizabeth said nothing but he felt her arms encircle his waist and her hands take hold of his cloak. And the way her breasts, those wonderful, sensitive, responsive breasts that had risen to tight peaks in his hands, pressed into his back. His cock rose until it nearly reached where she rested her hands. If she moved them a slight bit, she would touch him there. He shuddered at the thought, causing her to shift against him.

It was heaven and hell all in the same moment.

They traveled as long as they could, stopping only twice to refresh themselves. If they ran into more storms, they would be forced to delay locating Father Ceallach another night. James had no doubt that they would be pursued at some point—one did not break with the Earl of Douran on his own lands and not answer for it. So, each delay could be the one that allowed their plans to be thwarted.

Due to his unfamiliarity with the lands here, he'd overestimated the distance and the time needed to reach the village and the priest. It was midafternoon when they reached the first of the village buildings—a smithy from the sound and smell of it.

There would be time enough to stop at the inn for a true meal and to buy some necessities before seeking out the good father and finishing this escapade. Then they could begin the marriage based on deception and dishonor.

Dougal and the men reached the peak of what should be the last hill before reaching the road that James must have taken with his sister. It was the only road into the village to the south and then through onto Glasgow. And just beyond the village lay the old priest's dwelling and small chapel.

Their luck had held for the storms that had plagued the land all of the day before, had broken apart in the skies above and eventually the nearly full moon's light showed the way. Stopping only to relieve themselves, they ate or drank as they needed while they rode, intent on stopping the Murrays' heir from taking advantage of his sister and to return him to face the earl's justice in the matter. They could rest once he was their prisoner.

Niall spied the shieling just before they reached it, for it was hidden from above by the turf roof and the way it was built into the side of the hill. That protected it from the worst of the winds and created a small, sheltered place where animals could be covered. As they pulled to a halt, Shaw pointed out the tree that had burned, struck by lightning most likely.

The shieling looked undisturbed and his hope that they would catch the two inside faded as he untied the rope and pulled the door open. It was empty. Dougal walked inside, waving off the others, and he took in all the signs of a recent use. What struck him as he had pulled open the door was the unmistakable, musky odor of sex.

Christ! The man had already taken Elizabeth. He was too late to save her from shame. He kicked the stool near his feet, sending it crashing into the wall. It was not as satisfying as he'd hoped. But, he would get satisfaction when they caught up with the pair. Young James Murray would pay.

He strode out and mounted his horse. They were on the right path and would catch up with them. He only hoped it was before they reached the priest and made this man's crime into something too difficult to correct. Dougal motioned to Niall and Shaw and they rode down to the packed dirt path...and on toward the village and his sister.

# EIGHT

Elizabeth pulled another piece off the roasted quail and put it on her wooden trencher. She did not realize how hungry she was until the innkeeper's wife began putting plates on their table. The bird, a thick stew of mutton and vegetables, another with cheese and bread. All smelled delicious and could not be resisted after the plain oatcakes of this morn.

A younger woman, mayhap the innkeeper's daughter, hovered around Jamie, filling his cup with ale as soon as he drank some and offering him whatever he needed. It did not take too much thinking to understand what she offered and only after several dark glares did the girl go away and tend to others.

Jamie did not seem to notice her untoward attentions. His gaze moved between his cup, the plates of food and his own trencher. He hardly spared her a glance, so lost in thought he was. So, deciding that she would rather face his anger than this polite attitude, she spoke to him of the one topic neither had mentioned.

"I wonder what happened to Ciara."

"Ciara?" He drank deeply from his cup.

"Just because you—we—left, it does not mean that she married or will marry Tavis." She sipped from her own cup and then added, "Or that the earl would permit such a marriage."

James studied her then, before answering. "I had not thought of that. Tavis would not be a suitable choice for a woman of such wealth and connections."

"Nor am I one for a man such as you."

He let out a breath then and met her gaze directly for the first time they'd lain together and he discovered her secret.

"Nay, you would not be someone considered when my parents were looking for a suitable bride." He took her hand then and entwined their fingers, sending tiny bursts of pleasure and sadness through her. "But you are the woman I chose. We will make the best of this bad beginning."

There was the problem—she did not want to make the best of this. That was what she would have done had James married Ciara. Elizabeth would have remained at home, mourned the loss of the man she loved and the forced loss of her closest friend. For in marrying, James and Ciara would ensure Elizabeth's alienation from them. She would not have been able to bear watching them.

She thought that that situation would have been the worst thing to come from this three-sided relationship, but listening to James now, Elizabeth knew there was worse.

This would be worse—to marry the man she loved and wanted because he felt trapped. It would eventually change whatever love he felt for her into complacency and forbearance, one for the other. But what choice did she have now? What choice did he have? To act honorably and return her to Lairig Dubh, not married? To return to marry Ciara? Her head ached from the uncertainty of it all.

Her appetite fled her then, so she wiped her hands on the cloth given her and waited for James to finish eating. He asked the innkeeper's wife to wrap the food that they did not eat so they could take it with them and she carried it off to do that. Elizabeth stood and watched as James got directions to where the priest lived. Once that was accomplished and a few of James's coins paid for their meal, they walked out onto the road.

"It did not sound far," she said.

"Not far at all. About a mile farther on that road," he said, pointing out a smaller path that would lead out of the village, but in a different direction than the main one.

"Could we walk part of the way? I do not think I could on the back of a horse right now."

He glanced overhead to gauge the position of the sun and how much daylight they had left before dusk would fall. There should be plenty of time, so he nodded and held out his hand. Though certain she wanted to rage at him, she accepted his hand in hers and they fell into step with the horse behind them.

They'd left the village, which was fading from sight behind them, but there was still no sign of the priest's abode or the small church Lady MacLerie had mentioned was his. It could not be much farther.

Before they caught sight of anything in the thick forest that surrounded them, the sound of galloping horses grew louder. Someone or several people approached at a fast speed, though only the sound of it echoed yet. James released Elizabeth's hand and drew the sword he'd placed next to the saddle. He wore a lethal dagger in his boot, if needed, but he hoped this was someone anxious to find the priest. Kin or kith near death and in need of the Last Rites?

Or not, for now he could see two horsemen riding toward them. Hoping she had not been seen, he pushed her toward the trees.

"Hide, Elizabeth," he said, moving away from her to take any attention. "Now, lass. Hide."

She hesitated for only a moment before fleeing into a thick stand of bushes just a few paces off the road. Once she hid from sight, James mounted and turned to face the men. From the color of their garments, they were dressed in the Highland manner and wore the MacLerie hunting plaids.

Fate...and the earl, it would seem, had caught up with them. James held the sword low and ready as the two men slowed and stopped near him.

"Where is she?" the red-haired one called out. "What have you done with Elizabeth?" Although his understanding and speaking of Gaelic was not the best, he comprehended the questions. Only when the man glared at him did he recognize him from a similar expression that Elizabeth often wore when angry.

"Dougal?"

"Aye, Murray. I am Dougal MacLerie. And I ask you again, what have you done to my sister?"

Before he could answer, another man approached from the other direction and positioned himself to block any attempt at escape. Even if he wanted to try, the man held a bow with an arrow nocked and ready and aimed at him. Hemmed in, he had no place to go. He heard her moving through the bushes just before she appeared at the edge of the road.

"Dougal! What are you doing?" she called out to her brother first. "Niall! Put down that bow!"

Elizabeth stood with her hands on her hips and that mutinous expression that mirrored the one her brother yet wore. James noticed that neither answered her or took their eyes off of him. He lowered his sword slightly and waited.

It was not long in coming. A nod from Dougal sent the man closest to him riding at James. But he was not the target—Elizabeth was, and he was too far from her to stop it. The warrior leaned over and scooped her up, tossing her over his legs in spite of the fight she gave. With one arm across her back to hold her there, the man turned his horse and rode away. She was still screaming—curses now—as they disappeared from sight over the rise in the road.

She was not in danger, but James was certain he was.

Dougal and Niall stayed in position, on either side of him, so he could not defend himself or fight one of them without the other being free to attack him. So, he waited to see what they had planned.

Niall remained some distance away when Dougal launched his attack. Charging him directly, James was forced to turn and ride toward Niall. As he did, Niall aimed the bow and James knew he would be struck in the leg by it. He stopped his horse and jumped from it, using it as cover while Dougal approached, driving his horse away.

Breathing heavily, James stood in the middle of the road awaiting his fate. Would they kill him now? The murderous look in Dougal's eyes said aye. Niall seemed to be waiting for Dougal to act, for he never moved from his place or took his aim off his target. James took a deep breath as Dougal charged him now, for there was no hope of outrunning a man on a horse. At the last moment, he ducked low and turned away, but Dougal freed his foot from the stirrup and kicked him to the ground.

James's landed facedown in the dirt and before he regained his feet, Dougal was there, sword in hand and murder in his eyes, ready to strike him down with the lethal Highland claymore he carried.

"Dougal," Niall said. James had not seen the other man's approach, but he sat on his horse just a few yards away. "Your orders."

"Aye, Niall. I know the earl's orders." Dougal spit on the ground then. "He's to be brought back alive to Lairig Dubh." Dougal turned toward Niall and tossed the huge sword to him. Niall caught it with ease and nodded to Dougal. "I do not need my sword to show this cur that he should not have involved my sister in his plans." Dougal climbed down from his horse and handed the reins to Niall, too. "Now, outlander swine, let me show you how a Highlander answers insult."

No more words were spoken. Once Dougal launched at him, James could barely think. It felt like the man had eight arms and legs. The blows came from every direction and James recognized the pure fury in the attack. He'd held his own while fighting Tavis, but Tavis did not have righteous anger in his soul as Dougal did.

After the first punches and kicks, Dougal slowed the attack.

No need to rush the punishment this dog would get at his hands. Once Murray's vision was blocked by the blood pouring from a gash on his head and from the swelling from several of Dougal's punches to his face, Dougal taunted him. Pushing him down from behind, he ground his face into the dirt of the road and punched him in the back.

There would be bruises aplenty on the morrow.

Oh, he was not unscathed but at least he would be standing when this was over. Only when Niall called out his name, did he stop. He trusted his friend to call a halt before the man died. After one more very satisfying punch to his face, Dougal walked away.

He took the skin of water from his horse and after taking a mouthful of it to rinse out the blood, he dowsed his head and face with some. Then he washed Murray's blood from his knuckles and hands. Niall brought Murray's, or rather the earl's, horse over and together they threw the unconscious man over the saddle, tying his hands and legs to each other under the horse's belly to keep him in place.

As they rode to catch up with Shaw and Elizabeth, who would be waiting north of the village, Dougal wondered what the earl would do with the man...and with his sister. It was near full-dark by the time they reached the agreed-to place, but Shaw had a fire built and was waiting for them. They dismounted and walked closer, seeing the cuts and scrapes all over Shaw's face and neck and hands.

"What happened?" Dougal asked, glancing around the clearing.

"Your sister did not wish to leave," Shaw said, touching one ugly gash on his neck.

"Where is she?" Dougal could hear noises but could not see Elizabeth.

"Over there," Shaw said. "It seemed the best way to keep her and myself safe." Dougal followed him across the clearing where Shaw led.

Elizabeth sat at the base of a tree, her hands and feet tied together and rope binding her to the tree. A length of cloth was tied around her face, gagging her mouth, though not stopping her from trying to scream at him. Dougal knelt in front of her and removed the cloth.

"Are you hurt, Elizabeth? Did he harm you?" He searched her face for any sign of injury from whatever Murray did to her.

"Shaw did not hurt me, Dougal. I am calmed down now, you can untie me." She lifted her arms as much as the other ropes allowed, clearly expecting him to cut her free. He did nothing.

"I meant Murray. His note said he kidnapped you from Lairig Dubh. Did he...?" Dougal paused, thinking of the smell of the shieling. "Did he force himself on you?"

"You are a fool if you think he forced himself on me, Dougal. I did not think you a fool before." Her eyes narrowed. "Untie me. Let us go."

"I have my orders, from the earl. We are to bring you back to Lairig Dubh."

She stared at him then and said nothing.

"Tell me, Elizabeth," he insisted. "The earl will want to know what happened."

When her chin lifted just a bit and her lower lip edged out, he knew he'd lost this battle. Stubborn to the core, she did as she pleased and answered to no one when she wore this expression. His anger drained from him and, pushing her tangled hair from her eyes, he asked his sister what he needed to know.

"Are you well, lass? Just tell me that much," he said quietly so that none of the others heard.

The tears welling in her eyes worried him, but she blinked them away quickly and nodded. Turning away, she would not say anything else. Until she noticed Murray's body strung over the horse.

"Dougal, what have you done now?" she said in a tone that nearly shouted at him. "Untie me." She began to fight the ropes and, with the way Shaw tied his knots, it would only make them tighten more. "I beg you, Dougal. Niall. Shaw." She looked at each of them. "Let me see to him. Please."

Dougal just shook his head and walked away from her. Her reactions to seeing Murray as they'd left him explained much to him—more than he wished to know. Elizabeth had not been kidnapped. She had not been forced. She had been a willing participant in this folly and she would need to pay a steep price for contributing to her loss of honor. The earl would determine that once they got back home.

And she was mistaken if she thought she gave the orders. With a nod of his head, he directed the others to follow him. In a few minutes, they'd untied Murray, laid him on the ground on the other side of the clearing and bound his hands and feet so he could not move when he did wake. When he glanced in her direction, he found her straining against the ropes to see what they were doing.

They would stay here for the night. Now that they had Murray, they did not have to rush back to Lairig Dubh.

Only after he tossed a blanket over Elizabeth and took one for himself, assigning each of his men a guard shift through the night, did he allow himself to feel the exhaustion and the pain that coursed through his body. A few hours of rest and he'd be fine. With a clearer head, he would deal with Elizabeth and her lover in the morn.

# NINE

Although she was tied to a tree and worried to death about Jamie, Elizabeth did fall asleep several times during that long night. She noticed when Niall changed places with Shaw and then when Dougal took over. She saw the sky begin to lighten as the sun threatened to rise and she watched as the clouds thickened overhead and rolled ominously above them.

All night long she tried to remember the secret to Shaw's knots. She'd been successful in loosening them when she was younger and her brother and his friends liked to play tricks on her and the other girls. Fighting them tightened them, so she tried to slide her fingers loose by easing her hands to and fro within the intricate loops. A dagger. What she wouldn't give for a good, sharp dagger that could cut through the rope and cut off a few dangly bits from her brother's body, too!

She should feel embarrassed and humiliated, but instead she felt murderous. Dougal had purposely ordered Shaw to take her away so she could not interfere with his plans to beat Jamie to within an inch of life. The earl would never have made such an order and Elizabeth was certain that that part had been Dougal's decision.

Peering across the clearing, she tried to see if Jamie yet slept. His face was bloodied and swollen. He had not moved since they dropped him there. She needed to see to his injuries before Dougal tried to travel back to Lairig Dubh. Elizabeth was concentrating so hard on freeing herself and on seeing how Jamie fared that she never heard Dougal's approach from behind her.

"Here," he said, holding out a skin to her. "Drink."

Nothing else. No apologies for tying her to a tree and leaving her all night. She was thirsty enough that she would have taken it from him—until she saw the bloody splashes on his hands and arms.

Jamie's blood.

With the increasing light from the sun, she could see that Jamie must have fought back, for Dougal was a bit bruised about the face. And he grimaced as he leaned over to her.

Good. She hoped he was suffering for what he'd done.

"Connor ordered you to beat him?" she asked.

"Connor ordered me to bring him back alive. I but

treated him to the anger of a brother for the mistreatment of his sister." He held out the skin again.

"'Twas not your place to do so, Dougal. I did not need you to avenge my honor."

If he had lived in the village during that previous incident, he would have done the same thing. She tried not to be too angry at him for he did not realize he was returning her to face shame once more before the earl and that it would end with her complete disgrace and exile from their family.

Worse, her parents would bear this shame, too. The earl might be a worldly man and intelligent and willing to forgive a young, stupid and naive girl's misstep once. But this time would push him into harsher actions against her. The only problem was that she could not explain it to Dougal without first exposing her misjudgment.

She could not bear to have her brother look at her with disappointment in his gaze. That she would not do.

"Drink and I'll take you so you can see to your needs. You must have to..." He motioned off to the ground, where he and the other men could so easily see to theirs.

"I would see to Jamie, Dougal. Please."

They had reached a point familiar to both of them. Their innately stubborn natures brought them to it many, many times and it became a joke of a sort between them. Who would give in this time? If she did, would it soften his refusal to let her help Jamie? She must take the chance, for his sake.

She held out her hands and he placed the skin in them, pulling the stopper free. Elizabeth lifted it up and drank slowly. After a few mouthfuls, she handed it back to him. He sealed it and slung it over his shoulder. When she held out her hands to him, he loosened the knots and the ropes dropped off.

It only took a moment to free her feet, but she wobbled as she tried to stand. Dougal grabbed her by the arm and waited until she got her feet beneath her. He tugged her in the other direction from where she wanted to go and walked with her into the trees, looking for a place out of sight of the other men. When they were behind enough trees so she would not be seen, he released her.

"I will wait here. Go, see to your needs."

She did not take long, once her legs stopped burning from lack of movement, she finished her task and returned to her brother. He walked next to her on the way back to the clearing, allowing her to walk without holding her. So, when they reached the others, she paused and waited, hoping he would let her go to Jamie. He took her by the arm and she thought he meant to tie her up again, but they walked on past the tree and across the clearing to where he lay.

Elizabeth tried not to cry before them, but the tears streamed down her cheeks when she saw the damage her brother had wrought on Jamie.

There was a deep gash that began on his forehead and ran into his hair, which still bled. His left eye was swollen shut and his jaw was mottled with bruises. His lip was split in the center and dried blood covered his face and neck. From the strange way his fingers fell, she thought he might have broken two or three of them on his left hand. It was all she could do not to fall to her knees and wail like a *bean-shithe* singing her song of death. Elizabeth took a deep breath and told Dougal what she needed.

Though he stood there silently watching her, he nodded and left, returning a few minutes later with water, her other shift to use for bandages and some whisky for cleaning the wounds and helping with his pain. She proceeded to clean the wounds she could find, even tearing open the bloodied shirt to find more bruises and cuts on his chest. His head and face were the worst and she thought the gash was deep enough to need stitches— stitches she did not have.

It took her some time and all the while the three men stood off a bit watching and saying nothing. Did they hear her prayers as she whispered them to the Almighty? Elizabeth had helped her mother tend the sick but this was beyond that. What worried her the most was that through it all, through the poking and prodding and cleaning, Jamie never moved or made a sound.

She called Niall over when she needed help wrapping the long strips of linen, torn from her shift, around his chest to support what she thought might be broken or badly bruised ribs. Finally finished, she gathered up the cloths she'd used and handed the water skin back to Dougal.

"The rains are coming again and he will need shelter, Dougal. At least until he wakes." She tried to soften her voice so it did not sound like an order, but she knew it did. And she did not care. "If he wakes."

All three men paled at her words. Dougal took them aside to talk amongst themselves and she knelt at Jamie's side, holding his battered hand in hers. Niall walked away first and then Dougal returned to her.

"Niall is going to the village. There was an unused cottage there and he will make arrangements. Since these people pay their rents to the MacLerie, it should be easy to arrange."

"My thanks, Dougal," she said. Then she watched as he frowned and stared at her as though trying to decipher a puzzle.

He did not try to move her from her place next to Jamie, so she remained there, watching him closely for any sign of waking. Each hour that passed with him asleep brought the danger closer. He could not die because of her. Because of her brother's need to settle a score. Because of her past indiscretions.

Sometime much later, Elizabeth's stomach grumbled, reminding her of how much time had passed since her last meal. Though she did not want to leave his side, she climbed to her feet and walked to where they'd piled all the bags from the horses. Finding the right sack, she found the leftover oatcakes, quail, cheese and bread. She kept one oatcake and gave the rest to Dougal and Shaw.

She leapt up at the sound of Niall's return. When she stood and saw that his horse now pulled a wooden cart behind it, she thought there was some hope for Jamie. Niall drove the horse into the clearing and held onto the reins while Dougal and Shaw lifted Jamie and placed him in the back. When they tossed the bags in, she arranged a couple of them under Jamie's head to absorb most of the bumpiness of the rough road on the way back to the village.

The small cottage sat just before the village, farther into the forest so it was not easily seen from the road. Niall turned the horse down a small, almost-hidden path and it appeared after a few minutes. Trying to keep her bearings, Elizabeth thought it might have been about a quarter mile. Niall helped her down from the bench of the cart and she went to see what the cottage looked like inside. The winds whipped her hair loose and she had to gather it in her hands to keep it out of her face. She leaned down to enter through the lower door.

Not as tiny as the shieling, but not very big, the cottage had three rooms—one main living area with a hearth built into one wall, another smaller, windowless room suitable as a storage room and one bedroom, this with one small window high in the back wall. Escape would be impossible from this cottage, which from his smile, Dougal must have realized at the same moment she had.

The good thing was that it was clean, with no rodents or other creatures hiding in it as usually happened with unused crofts. And, as the skies opened and the rains poured down, it did not leak. She'd managed to make a pallet out of some blankets on the floor of the storage chamber for Jamie, and Niall and Shaw carried him inside just as the storm began.

The men also brought in supplies and foodstuffs, a small keg of whisky and another of ale. From the looks of it, Dougal took Jamie's injuries seriously and understood it could be days before he could travel.

"I borrowed what I could and bought some. The innkeeper provided me with a griddle pan and some pots and plates. They recognized me as the earl's man and said he would get whatever we needed," Niall explained as he set out the goods he'd returned with. "We can return everything when we leave and pay for what we use."

She walked into the smallest room and checked on Jamie before beginning to organize the food and supplies in the cooking area. He lay unmoving as before and seemed no worse for the short, though bumpy journey here. Her brother and the others would expect her to cook while they stayed here. Elizabeth wondered if Dougal yet remembered how badly she cooked.

The rains continued through the rest of the day. The innkeeper had sent along another quail, so she boiled it to make broth for him and the others would eat the rest of it. Tempted to cook the way she had at home to hide her skills, she decided against it. So, she made simple foods to feed them.

The day passed slowly for her. She spent most of her time sitting with Jamie, hoping that he would wake so she could explain things to him. The earl knew the truth about her past and would certainly not force Jamie into a marriage knowing that. If nothing else, she had decided to plead that to the earl when they returned and hopefully Connor would be content banishing her from Lairig Dubh and returning Jamie to face his parents' wrath.

That night she and Dougal shared the bedchamber, with Dougal sleeping across the place in front of the door. Niall and Shaw slept in the main room. Elizabeth prayed for many things that night, but mostly she prayed that Jamie would wake up.

Darkness and agony swirled around him, making it impossible for him to see anything. He struggled against it, fighting his way through the waves of pain only to face more. His body hurt, his head hurt, but worse was the anguish that pierced his heart when he remembered how he'd treated Elizabeth.

Her eyes, carrying that secret shame deep within them, pleading with him for understanding. And he failed her. He professed his love and ignored his pride. He needed to tell her.

Elizabeth! He tried to call to her but she faded away.

He would never let her go. He would never let her face her family, the laird, and be subjected to censure of any kind. She was his.

Her voice echoed in his head then and he pushed his way to reach her. But no matter what he did, he could not seem to make her hear him. Over and over, hour after hour, he called for her. Her touch on his hand or his arm or his head soothed him. When he tried to reach for her, his body would not do what he wanted. His eyes would not even open so he could see her.

Had Dougal hurt her? Had he punished her for his sins?

With all his might, against the terrible wall of pain, he pushed, trying to get a sound through to her. Then exhausted, he fell back into the black depths of unconsciousness.

His last thought was for her, a prayer that she would forgive him for failing her so badly.

# TEN

At first, she thought she was dreaming or imagining it.

Elizabeth moved the tallow candle closer and watched carefully, but now there was no sign of movement. Two days and nights had passed and he remained deeply unconscious. Dougal even sent for one of the old women of the village, one who had some skills in healing and treating the sick, but she said she could do nothing more for him.

Head injuries, she whispered to Dougal believing Elizabeth could not hear her, were the least predictable of all. But, she warned him that this deep sleep was lasting too long and not a good sign. With a promise to visit again in a few days and after leaving a few potions and concoctions behind in case she had need of them, the old woman waddled her way along the road back to the village, refusing any attempt to take her by cart.

As had become her practice these last few days, Elizabeth sat at his side and spoke quietly to him. Most times she simply repeated prayers so that he could hear them. Other times, she told him of her childhood and good stories about Dougal so he would know her brother was not just an evil person. And sometimes, when the men were outside the cottage, she spoke of her love for him and her failures.

But mostly, she prayed she would have a chance to make things right between them.

Old Muireall approved of feeding him some of the broth Elizabeth had made, so a couple times a day, she sat behind him, with his head resting on her chest, and dribbled spoonfuls of liquid into his mouth. She could coax it down his throat, much more successfully than the first few times she'd tried. Now, he swallowed more of it than they both wore.

The outside door opened and she waited for word of what the men had discussed. When no one approached, she walked to the chamber door and eased it open. All three stood there, silent now that she'd opened the door. Dougal motioned to her to come out, so she stepped out and pulled the door behind her.

"If he does not wake in another two days, I am sending Niall back to Lairig Dubh with word of his condition," he said.

Elizabeth nodded at his grim announcement. For

Dougal to send word to the earl that exposed that he had lost his temper and caused Jamie's condition was a serious admission to make. He would be in trouble for disobeying the laird's commands, losing whatever status he might have and being humiliated among his clan.

How had things gone so wrong?

She went back into the chamber to watch over Jamie, but dissolved into tears when she knelt next to him. Everything had gone wrong and a simple desire to be together had now ruined more lives than she could count—and might even cost Jamie his.

All for love? She thought love would be the answer to their problems, but instead pursuit of it seemed to cause all their problems. Standing by while Ciara married him could not be worse than the mayhem and damage following their own desires had wrought. Mayhap being content in marriage was enough and seeking a grand adventure of the heart just brought pain?

She leaned her head down and let her grief and worry out for the first time. Praying that his life would be spared, she bargained with the Almighty, offering up all manner of possible sacrifices if only...if only...

"Dinna greet, lass."

Low and raspy, she nearly did not recognize his voice, but as he touched her head, tangling his fingers in her unbound hair, she knew he was truly awake. Elizabeth lifted her head and looked into his eyes for the first time in days.

"Nothing can be as bad as that," he whispered to her. He had no idea of how bad things were at that moment. Happy that he was waking up, she smiled through her tears.

"Not now that you are awake," she said. Without thinking about anything else, she leaned over and kissed him. Careful not to press too hard against his torn lip, she only touched her mouth to his for a moment. Realizing he must be parched, she sat up and reached for the cup she kept there, always ready for him. "Here now, sip this," she said, lifting his head so he could take some.

She did it in small steps, until he'd emptied the cup. When she let his head rest back, he reached out and took hold of her hand, squeezing it for a moment.

"Elizabeth, we must talk," he said. His eyes began to droop and she knew he was falling asleep again, this time into a normal sleep so she did not fear for him. "I have to tell you..."

He never finished his words. She did not care for there would be time now to sort it all out. After watching him for several more minutes, she left the chamber to tell Dougal the news.

With the news that he'd wakened, everyone's mood lightened and their meal included a bit of conversation that no one had felt like having at previous meals. After eating and cleaning up, Elizabeth reached for the latch to his door. Dougal stepped between her and the chamber, stopping her from entering.

"Go now, Elizabeth, and get some rest."

"I want to sit with him, Dougal. If he wakes..."

"When he wakes, I will call you. But, if you do not get some sleep, you will make yourself sick and be of no good to him or anyone."

When he crossed his arms over his chest, she knew she'd lost this argument. Nodding, she went into the bedchamber and lay down on the pile of blankets there. Only planning to sleep for a short time, Elizabeth was surprised when morning's light greeted her as she woke.

Dougal watched the steely determination in his sister and understood what, or who, caused it. Murray had not forced her in any way—Elizabeth was deeply in love with him. As he observed her care of him over the last several days, it was a fact he could not miss. Not even while his temper still held sway over him. Not even when the man's death seemed imminent. And not even now when the news he'd awakened lifted her spirits.

He sat with his back against the wall inside the small chamber, drinking some whisky and thinking on how this would all go and not liking any of it. His first time in command and it was a debacle. He'd lost his temper within seconds of encountering the two of them and nearly beaten Murray to death. He was not one to shy away from a good fight or even from killing when it needed be done, but the results of this lack of control sickened him.

Connor expected obedience from everyone who served him. Duncan and Rurik had tried to warn him, but he was too bent on avenging what he thought was Murray's dishonoring of his sister to keep his temper under control.

Taking another swallow of the *uisge beatha* he considered his choices in how to carry out his orders and how they would affect his sister and the man before him. Her earlier indiscretion aside, she was his younger sibling, the only one to live through childhood, and though he and his friends tormented her endlessly, their bond was unbreakable. She probably wished him in hell right now, he knew that from the glare she gave him from time to time.

The last time Elizabeth had fallen from honor, it was because she was too sweet and too young to know a man's game...and because he was not there to watch over her. It would have taken him no more than a breath to see the craven bastard's plan and put an end to it—if he'd been there. But he was training and living elsewhere and Elizabeth had been drawn in with the man's pretty words and promises. She did not think he knew about it but he did.

He could not fail her this time.

So, when word spread that she'd been taken by Murray, that he'd forced her to leave with him, he knew his chance had come. The smell of recent sex in the shieling just proved Murray's guilt to him and he'd attacked the man—for his own failure once more.

From Connor's comments to his wife, he fully expected Murray to marry his sister. Actually, it sounded as though he expected they would already be married by the time they were found. The chieftain had allowed his friend Tavis to marry Ciara, though in many ways, it was not an acceptable match. Ciara Robertson was higher in status, connected to powerful families in Scotland and wealthier than any woman Dougal could think on. And it was her wealth, not her husband's.

Now that he'd time to think on it, mayhap Connor waited to give Murray time to marry Elizabeth? The earl knew where they were heading because Lady MacLerie told them about the priest. By giving them an entire day before sending someone after them, Connor knew they would have done the deed before being found. Which would give Connor less control over separating them once they were returned. A valid marriage, even in the Old Church style, was legitimate and hard to break.

But the storms arrived and delayed them in getting to the priest. And that gave him a chance to catch up with them before that marriage could happen.

He drank down the last of the whisky in his cup and thought on all of this. It was moot until Murray was able to travel, so there was time aplenty to make decisions about his orders. Dougal was about to close his eyes and get some sleep when Murray moved, shifting and moaning out his sister's name as he did.

The man, though a Lowland nobleman and not trained as he'd been by the best warriors in the Highlands, could inflict pain with his punches, too. Dougal had been impressed, as had Niall, in his ability to last as long as he had and to land some bruising blows. His own ribs ached even now. Pouring more whisky in his cup from the keg at his side, he went over and crouched next to him.

"Here, Murray," he said, lifting the man's head. "This will help with the pain." Although he did not resist, Murray eyed him with suspicion as he drank it down. "I am not trying to poison you. If you think to marry my sister, her cooking may very well do that for you." Dougal let Murray's head rest back down.

"She told me as much," Murray said, as he slid his hand down over his tightly bound ribs.

Though now that he thought on the matter of Elizabeth's cooking, Dougal realized that none of the meals she'd made for them had sickened any of them. Hmmm.

"What are you going to do, Dougal?"

How many times could he fail his sister before doing what was best for her? That was the true question in all this, was it not? And all he knew was that he did not know the answer yet. Pouring himself another wee dram and drinking it down, Dougal shrugged.

"Get some rest, Murray. We will talk in the morn."

Knowing the man was well-enough, Dougal rose and walked out into the main room. And laying himself down in front the chamber's door, he went to sleep, wondering just what the bloody hell he would do.

James listened as Dougal left the chamber.

Every part and bit of him hurt, but he was alive. Until he woke to the sound of Elizabeth crying, he did not know if he would ever wake again. He'd actually thought at first that she was sobbing because he'd died. The pain seeped into his mind and he knew that only being alive could hurt this much.

What a fool he'd been! Not speaking on things that mattered with the woman he loved was likely the stupidest thing he'd done in his life. For a time, while drifting in that blackness he thought would lead him to death, he prayed for a second chance with her. To make things right.

He did not know how, he only knew to the core of his soul that he must keep her with him and keep her from further humiliation.

As he drifted back to sleep, he thought on how he could do it and realized the only way was to kidnap her from her brother and get to the priest before they could be stopped. He laughed then and it made his ribs spasm with pain at the movement. The pain reminded him of all the reasons that would be impossible.

But, he would find a way to do it, to prove his love to her and to keep her at his side for the rest of their lives. If he died trying, so be it, however he would try.

For Elizabeth.

# ELEVEN

"Dougal!" she cried out.

She'd opened the door to the chamber and found Jamie on his hands and knees, heaving.

"Dizzy," he whispered. "So dizzy."

"Move away, Elizabeth," her brother ordered.

She jumped out of his way and watched as he and Shaw lifted Jamie by gripping his arms and moved him back to sit against the wall.

"Open your eyes and look at something," Dougal ordered. "And do not breathe too deeply. The dizziness should lessen that way."

Elizabeth met Jamie's gaze and held it as he took in some slow, shallow breaths as her brother had told him to do. When he smiled, a crooked one because of the injuries to his mouth and jaw, she knew he felt better.

"How did you know?" she asked Dougal.

"I've had my wits knocked about a few times," he replied as Shaw laughed. She suspected they'd done it together and that too much whisky was involved. "Rurik told me and it worked."

Rurik, the leader of all the MacLerie warriors, would know—he'd probably been the one giving these and other brash, young men thrashings that put them in their places...and addled their wits. Some unspoken message went between the men and Dougal took a step back and turned to her.

"Elizabeth, would you fill the bucket at the stream?"

"There is water in it already." She frowned as she looked from Dougal to Shaw and Jamie, all of whom looked at her with some expectation in the expression.

"Then, put more in it, lass," Shaw said.

They wanted her gone for some reason. Blaming it on general daft male behavior that had no rational explanation, she walked from the room, grabbed the bucket and left the croft. The steam cut closest to the village behind this dwelling, convenient for them, and it took her no time to reach it.

As she dipped the bucket in the cold water, fear struck her. Why did Dougal want her gone? What were they doing with or to Jamie? She dropped the bucket and ran back to the cottage.

Empty. All of them gone. She stepped to the door and listened, hoping to hear something, anything, that would tell her where they'd taken him. Low, grumbling tones echoed from off the side, where the trees thickened and blocked her view. Elizabeth followed the sounds, making her way there as quietly as possible. She crept from tree to tree, searching ahead for a sign they were near. Niall's laughter led her to them.

They stood side by side in a line with their backs to her. At first, it was not clear what they were doing and, quite happy to see Jamie standing on his own, she knew all was well. Until the unmistakable sound of liquid splashing on the ground in front of them told her what they were doing.

"'Tis red," Jamie said.

"It will clear in a few days," Dougal counseled. Niall and Shaw added a grunt in what seemed to be agreement.

"Is that what Rurik says?" she asked, unable to keep silent any longer.

To their credit, none of them turned. None moved from their places at all or looked any place except up at the trees, but she noticed that the splashing stopped.

"She does not follow directions well, does she, Dougal?" Jamie drawled out.

"She is leaving now," Elizabeth said, content now that they were seeing to mundane things and not going to kill him.

As she reached the stream and searched for the bucket, she also realized that the men, especially Dougal and Jamie, seemed to have some truce between them.

Dougal had not threatened Jamie since that first day and had asked her some thoughtful questions about what had happened to them—all the while avoiding anything to do with the mountainside shieling, which she knew he'd visited.

Walking back slowly so the men had time to finish their task, she was surprised to find Jamie outside alone. Though he wobbled a bit from side to side, he stood on his own. Elizabeth noticed that he could open both eyes now that some of the swelling had resolved. Taking a thorough look at him, the certain knowledge that she loved him raced through her.

And she knew she would be letting him go. It was the only way that the earl could save face over their insult— she would be exiled and Jamie would leave. She tried to smile but tears flowed instead.

Jamie held out one hand to her and held his breath as she walked right into his embrace. His chest and back screamed out and he waited for the pain to subside enough to take a breath. No matter how painful it was, he would not release her. Not now, not ever.

"Dougal said I might speak to you alone."

She raised her head and looked at him. He rubbed the tears from her cheeks and ran his fingers through her hair. It was not bound up or braided as she usually wore it but flowed over her shoulders like a curtain. When the image of her riding him, naked with her hair like a curtain around her, their bodies sweating from a lively bout of

110

lovemaking, caused him to shudder and his whole body to react, he realized two things. First, he was not dead. The second was that not even the pain was enough to stop him from craving her as he did.

And he loved her more than that.

Dougal appeared at that moment, carrying one of the stools from inside, then placing it in front of him. "Sit."

It was a good thought but one his battered body did not obey. Dougal then grabbed him under the arm and lowered him to it. Without another word, Elizabeth's brother walked away. Gathering his thoughts, he set out to explain his stupidity and to beg her forgiveness.

"Elizabeth," he began. She moved away from him and began to pace the area around them.

"Jamie," she said. "You must let me speak first."

She was so upset she was shaking and trembling and it tore his heart open to see her so overwrought. He nodded.

"When we return to Lairig Dubh, I will speak to Connor about releasing you. I know you are a man of honor, but I do not expect you to marry me now simply because you asked me to. That offer was based on deception and lies. My deception and my lies. Connor knows the truth and will not force you in this, I know."

Her words poured out much like the rains had, in torrents, never slowing, without pause. And under them, he could hear the pain and shame she carried with her. That Connor knew about whatever had happened did not surprise him. Connor kept a close watch on anything and anyone that affected the MacLerie clan or interests. He had informants and spies all over Scotland and he gathered information like squirrels gathered nuts— storing it all away for when it was needed.

But Jamie did not understand how it had happened. Oh, he understood that some man would lust after her and want her, but why had she allowed it?

"Did you love him?" The words blurted out of him before he even finished thinking them. That was what he wanted to know, for it would explain much.

She stopped then and stared at him, not misunderstanding what he wanted to know. Her hands, now held together and twisting with tension, revealed how painful this was for her.

"I would like to say aye, but it was something else entirely," she admitted. "He was worldly and handsome and he was interested in me. Not Ciara, as most men are. In me."

He could see her next to Ciara—the blond beauty, the great heiress, the woman fluent in languages and at ease among the king's court. Elizabeth was always at her side, to him the perfect foil for her accomplished friend— loyal, unassuming, quietly supporting her friend. He'd been blinded the same way, seeing only Ciara at first. Until he'd looked past her to Elizabeth and then he never looked back at Ciara the same way.

"Who was he?" If he ever met him, the beating he'd

had at Dougal's hands would be only the beginning. She shook her head, not ready or willing to share that with him.

"It matters not," she whispered. "The results were terrible. He boasted to one of Connor's men and we were brought to Connor to answer for our actions." She closed her eyes that second and he knew she was reliving her shame.

"What did Connor do?" Jamie was fascinated by how the powerful earl approached problems and solved them. Ruthless, but not mean-spirited. Intelligent, but practical. A good laird and man.

"When it was clear that a marriage was not possible, Connor erased what had happened. The man was banished from any MacLerie lands as well as Connor's allies, even some of his enemies for fear of antagonizing him, too. The only people who knew about it—my parents, the man who'd heard the boast and me—were warned never to speak of it again."

She met his gaze then and he knew the worst was yet to come. Shifting on the stool, he held out his hand to her and she sat next to him on the ground, not looking at him. He tangled his fingers, the ones not broken, in her hair, smoothing it from her face as she spoke.

"The waiting was the worst. To see if there would be a bairn. I could not keep it, so Connor said plans would be made if there was one. I have never prayed as much as I did those weeks until my courses finally came." She smiled softly at him then. "Well, not until these last days for you."

"So, a youthful mistake."

"That is what Connor called it. After some time had passed and he was certain there was no gossip about, he began allowing me to travel with Ciara. Since she was closely watched, so was I."

"He can be a wise man."

"Aye, he is. But when crossed, he is terrifying. And now, I have done that. I ruined his plans for Ciara's marriage to you."

"Elizabeth, we fell in love."

"And tried to run away."

"To marry, lass. An honorable estate that."

"It only shows my weakness and my bad judgment. If I beg him, I think he will let you go." He pushed to his feet then, straining every muscle to stand and not fall on his face once again.

"I am going to marry you, Elizabeth," he swore, pulling her to him. "You will be my wife." She pulled away and, damn his weakness, he could not stop her.

"I will not marry you because you think it is the only honorable way in this, Jamie. I will not let you marry me and then have to be content because it was the thing to do. I do not want contentedness between us," she said vehemently. "I thought I did. I thought Ciara was right in that regard, that a calm, reasonable marriage was the one to pursue, but now I know I could not accept it, for you or from you."

"I was being daft, Elizabeth. I know I do not want a contented marriage with you, either. I want a loving, screaming, fighting, greeting, making-peace, passion-filled marriage. And I want it with you and no other." He took a step toward her, reaching out to her. "As I laid there thinking I was going to die, all I worried about was that you would never forgive me for the way I treated you. For doubting you. For doubting our love."

She stared at his face, trying to understand his words. Why did he need to be forgiven? And how could he accept that she came to his bed used and impure? Elizabeth wiped the tears from her eyes and watched his face. She'd been a fool the first time, believing false promises and pretty words.

But this was Jamie. He was willing to lose everything for her. He suffered at her brother's hands and did not rebuke her for it. He loved her. She loved him. It should be simple.

It was so complicated.

Loving someone as much as she loved him was complicated.

But, in the end, all it took was for her to accept the hand he held out to her and take the first step toward him. Then she was in his arms, kissing him as he kissed her back, with little regard for his bruises and cuts.

"What will we do?" she asked when she could pull herself away from his mouth.

"I think I will have to kidnap you from your brother," he said in a low voice. "And this time we will be married before he finds us."

"When?" she asked, happy to be kidnapped by him.

"As soon as I can ride and before Dougal can take us back to Lairig Dubh."

Suddenly, he was sinking and she tried to grab onto him. His legs gave out and they ended up on the ground with no hope of her getting him to his feet once more. She realized he would not be able to kidnap her, nor ride for some days more.

"Only one thing," he whispered, for Dougal and Shaw were heading toward them. "I think I will need your help when the time comes." She frowned and shook her head, not understanding. "I do not think I can overwhelm all three of them and steal you myself. I may need your help," he teased with the truth now.

"I would be glad to help you," she said, laughing. Dougal and Shaw reached them and helped Jamie to his feet. He'd done too much his first time out of his pallet and it would take a toll on him now. Already he had a greenish tint in his cheeks and he stumbled as they walked him back into the croft.

She forced him to rest for a few hours knowing if he was well, he would fight it. Instead, he fell asleep as soon as his head touched the pallet. Kidnap her indeed!

Then at the evening meal, which Jamie joined them for, glancing with a question in his eyes every time he tasted something she'd cooked, Dougal announced his plans.

"We will return to Lairig Dubh in two days," he explained. "We'll take the easier road back, but it's time to return."

No one said a word through the rest of the meal. Jamie's strength gave out just after eating, so he went to his pallet. Though Dougal made them keep the door open when she was in the chamber with him, her brother did not restrict their movements otherwise. Just as she was leaving to seek her bed, he touched her leg, sending chills up through her.

If they married...

With a soft laugh, she shook herself from that path of thought. His injuries would prevent many things for a number of days.

"Tomorrow. It must be tomorrow," he whispered.

How would they escape when he could barely move? But, from his expression she knew he would do whatever needed be done to get away.

How could she help? She nodded and began to leave, but not before spying the two bottles that Old Muireall left for her use. She did not say anything to Jamie because she was not certain what she could do. Elizabeth spent most of the night trying to come up with a plan and by morning she realized that her reputation for bad cooking would come in handy.

# TWELVE

The first sign that something was wrong was the loud, gurgling noises that echoed through the main room. Everyone ignored them at first, but soon all three of the men who'd eaten the stew Elizabeth had made for their midday meal were affected in the same way.

James had eaten only a thick porridge made from oats, since Elizabeth recommended it to him to regain his strength. He'd almost ignored her advice until she glared at him from behind Dougal's back. Now, as the clear signs of impending distress grew stronger, he was glad he had.

Elizabeth, who had been cleaning the bedchamber and gathering her clothes while her brother and the others ate, entered the room then. She nodded with her head toward his chambers and he followed that advice, too. When she joined him on the pretense of helping him pack for the trip planned on the morrow, she wore a nefarious expression on her face.

"What did you do? Serve them spoiled meat?" he asked in a whisper.

"Spoiled meat? Nay," she said, gathering the bags she'd already packed and bringing them to the door. "I used Old Muireall's sleeping potion." She pointed to the bottle still on the table there. Her eyes grew wide and she shook her head, looking horrified.

"A sleeping potion? That was a great idea," he admitted. Easier to sneak away than to try to fight off the three warriors. If they slept or were at least groggy, they had a chance of escaping. "But the noises? Their stomachs?"

She faced him now and he knew something had gone wrong.

"I gave them her purgative by mistake, Jamie."

From the sounds in the other room now, she'd given them a large dose of a powerful purgative. Dougal began to wail. Soon, all three men were in the throes of the effects of the medicine. James grimaced at the sounds until he heard the door crash open and all three ran out.

"Well, you cannot change it now. They will be unable to follow us? For some time?" he asked her.

"For hours and hours," she said. "I never meant..."

"They've been in their cups before. It will not be much different from that. It gives us time to escape." He bent to grab the bags from the floor but could lift only one. "And we will need an excess of time, it seems."

"This will be more than that, Jamie. That medicine works in many ways." His own stomach clenched then as he realized her meaning.

"They will live?"

She nodded, then continued to gather the important things that he could not lift and followed his slow pace out into the main room. Still deserted, they walked through and out. The horses had been hobbled in a small area behind the cottage, but they had to pass by Dougal, Niall and Shaw, who now writhed on the ground, to reach them.

"You did this on purpose, did you not, Elizabeth?" Dougal asked between retching.

"Dougal, I used the wrong potion. I am sorry," she said as they walked by. "It will pass." He could feel the pain and guilt in her voice. "Just do not drink anything but water until it does."

"I was not taking you back to Connor, Elizabeth," her brother moaned to them. "We were returning alone." Any other questions were put aside as another wave of illness struck him.

James made his way to the horses and managed to get two of them saddled, but he was weak and sweating by the time he finished. To make it worse, the sounds from the three men were hard to ignore and soon he thought he would lose his meager meal, too. Elizabeth did not remain with her brother, instead she followed him back and helped him ready the horses.

It must have been an hour before he was able to mount the horse. First, they thought of riding together so she could support him. Then they discussed taking two horses to make better time once they left the area. In the end, they took two and they began with a very slow walk. Each step the horse took made his ribs feel like they were breaking again. Only the very tight bindings Elizabeth had placed this morn kept him upright.

When he felt like falling off and lying in the road, he thought of her. Concentrating on riding through the village, he ignored everything and everyone else they passed. James managed to get into the horse's rhythm and moved with it, so that each pace was not as jarring. Soon, they reached the place in the road where Dougal and the others had caught them.

He listened every moment for the sound of horses behind them and only when the priest's dwelling and small forest chapel came into view did he allow himself to think this might work. He heard Elizabeth at his side and continued until they reached the front of the cottage. James wanted to help Elizabeth down from her horse, but that was the last thought he remembered until he woke and found her and an old man staring down at him.

"Ah, here he comes," the old man said. "He is waking now." Elizabeth touched his face and nodded.

"This is Father Ceallach," she said. "We found him, Jamie."

His vision faded in and out for several minutes. The priest held a small skin to his mouth and James took a drink, coughing when the strongest whisky he'd ever tasted hit his throat. But then, the warmth of it reached his stomach and it felt good. Another swig and the skin disappeared.

"Ready, lad?" Father asked. But before he could answer aye or nay, the man gripped his arm and pulled him to his feet in one smooth motion. Stunned by the strength of the man, James pushed his hair out of his eyes and met a merry grin. "Come then, into the chapel."

With the priest on one side holding him up and Elizabeth on his other, James found himself in a small church. Smaller than he'd ever seen before. Only a stone altar and a crucifix decorated the empty space. And a small lamp sat burning on the altar.

"Elizabeth said you wish to marry," the priest said. "Is that your intention then?"

James nodded and received a frown in response from Father.

"You must speak the words, James Murray," he advised.

"Aye, Father, I wish to marry Elizabeth MacLerie," he said, meeting her gaze and seeing the love there.

"Elizabeth, is it your intention to take James Murray as your husband?"

"Aye," she said softly, taking his uninjured hand in hers. "I wish to marry James Murray."

"From the looks of you, lad, there are objections to this marriage? Who objects?" the priest asked. Although he did not want to reveal much, how could he lie to this priest? So, after Elizabeth nodded at him, he explained it simply.

"Connor MacLerie probably objects, but I have not asked him in the last five days. Elizabeth's brother has objections, as well." Would he refuse them the sacrament? Was this all for naught?

"And even in the face of those objections, you would take marriage vows?" Father looked at each of them. When they answered, they spoke as one.

"Aye."

He placed his gnarled hand on theirs and asked them some questions, waiting for each to answer before asking the next.

"Will you have each other from now until death?

"Will you be faithful onto each other and to no other?

"Do you promise to honor and obey your husband, Elizabeth?"

There was a longer pause then as his Elizabeth seemed to hesitate to promise that, but she smiled and accepted the duty.

"Do you promise to cherish and honor your wife, James?" He did not hesitate.

"Aye, Father. I will do that." The priest smiled then and placed his hand over their heads in a blessing.

"You have spoken your intention to marry and have said your vows to each other. In God's name then, you are now husband and wife in His Sight. God be with you both."

James stood in silence for more than a moment. After months of believing he would marry another woman, he was finally joined to the woman he loved. After choosing to defy his family and a powerful lord, they were married now and nothing could separate them. After living a life of following the rules and doing the right thing, passion and love had led him to her.

"Wife," he said, lifting her hand to his mouth and pressing his lips against it.

"Husband," she replied, turning his hand over and kissing his palm.

He would have reacted to such a kiss had the church not begun to spin and swirl around him. The only thing he saw was her face as he landed at her feet.

But, they were married and nothing else mattered.

It was their wedding night.

Elizabeth sat by the bed and watched him sleep. Considering that he could be dead several times over, she was content to be at his side. They'd been through more in this last week than she could have dreamt possible.

She must be a sinful person after all, for she sat here thinking on all the things they should be doing...all the things she wanted to do with him. When her body began to heat and ache in places he'd touched that night, she tried to think on something else.

Looking around for something to divert her attention, she found nothing in the old priest's cottage to stop her wayward thoughts. He lived simply in this one room, though the comfortable bed was unexpected. The best thing was that it was larger than most beds to accommodate the priest's large frame. She smiled thinking on his name—Ceallach—which meant warrior. From his size and strength, he must have served some earthly lord before becoming God's servant.

He'd carried Jamie here as though naught but a bairn and placed him in the bed. Then, saying he had to visit a sick villager, he gave them leave to stay here until he returned in two days. His larder held food and supplies, which he also told her to make free use of. His last bit of instruction—to close the door and windows and not open them to anyone—forced her to remember that her brother would come here. And he would be furious after what she'd done.

Especially if he meant what he claimed—that he did not plan to force their return to Lairig Dubh. Well, if he had shared that bit of information with her sooner, it could have saved all of them much pain and suffering. She doubted that Dougal, Shaw and Niall would think of it like that, especially since it would be hours before their bodies calmed and the retching and other effects stopped.

Would they come here looking or would they return to the earl directly? No matter now, they were married and would face whatever challenges came together.

When night fell and he slept on, she took off her gown and slipped into bed at his side. It should have felt strange to do so. It did not. She had undressed him already so she carefully slid closer to him, laying her head against his shoulder. Sometime in the night, she woke to find him staring at her.

"You are here?" he asked, lifting his hand up to caress her cheek. "I thought it might have been a dream."

"It happened. You spoke the words before the priest and we are married." She touched his face then, outlining his chin and mouth.

"Where exactly are we?"

She smiled. He'd been unconscious when Father brought him in here. "In Father Ceallach's cottage. He has gone off to visit some sick villagers and given us the use of it for two days."

"Two days? A generous man, he is," Jamie said.

Elizabeth could see that he was yet exhausted and in pain. Desire warred with practicality within her. Love won out and she leaned in and kissed him lightly.

"Rest now. I would have you able to enjoy what I have planned for you, husband." She felt his flesh rise and press against her hip. And she laughed.

"I am not dead," he said in a supremely masculine way.

If he would not have a care for himself, she would. She must. "Sleep now, Jamie. Heal. And if you feel this way in the morning, I will not stop you."

There was honest acceptance in his eyes so she knew part of him might be ready but the rest of him would suffer. He took her hand in his and held it on his chest. In only moments, he slept, telling her how right she'd been.

They had the rest of their lives together and surely one night's delay meant nothing.

In the morning, he proved to her that neither he, nor the rest of him, was dead.

# THIRTEEN

*Three months later*

Elizabeth was having the most marvelous dream.

Jamie kissed her body and teased her to excitement with his mouth and hands. There was no place on her or in her that he had not touched and loved since their marriage. Now, she ached and throbbed. She was on fire from his caresses. She lay on her back and opened herself up to him. Whatever he wanted to do, she would do it.

Not wanting to wake up from such a wondrous, hot dream, she kept her eyes closed tightly as he created that ache deep inside her that she did not want eased...yet. She would want his mouth there, in that scandalous way she'd never dreamt possible, licking her deep between her legs, suckling on that place that would make her scream.

And scream she did as her body wound tighter and tighter and tighter, and then released. Even as she cried out in the pleasure of this release, he began it anew with his fingers moving there as he skimmed his mouth over her body, kissing and laving her breasts on his path to her face. The musky taste of her own essence on his mouth forced her to open her eyes.

It was not a dream.

"Good morning to you, wife," he whispered as he bit her neck gently. The feel of it made her arch against him as though a cord connected places within and he pulled on it with each touch and taste. "I wondered if you would sleep through all of it."

"I think I like being awakened this way, husband," she said, her voice rough from the first release. His fingers did not relent, not giving a moment for her body to cool.

"I know. You asked me to do it."

She laughed then, unsure of whether she had or had not. He rolled her to her side so he could kiss her neck and use his teeth on that sensitive spot she liked him to bite. Elizabeth followed his whispered directions until he lay behind her, with his fingers still there, rubbing and making her want more. Soon, she could not laugh or speak. He used her own desires, telling her what he wanted to do to her, with her, on her, in her, until she lay panting and sweating against him.

He lifted her leg over his and entered her from behind, making her gasp at his speed and depth. With his hand wrapped around her, tormenting the already heated flesh there and his cock plunging deep from behind, she went limp in his arms as he pushed her to another peak. Just as she fell apart with her second release, he slid his arm around her and lifted her onto her knees.

Still deep within her, touching her core and making her scream again, he leaned over her, his chest against her back, one hand twisting the length of her hair in his fist and pulling her head back to him and exposing her neck to him. His mouth was hot, his teeth grazing the skin and seeking the tender spot again, knowing what it did to her.

He never stopped moving or touching or thrusting within her. It hurt to breathe, every place felt so wet and ready, she wanted him to make it happen. Pushing back and down against his cock to move him deeper, she heard him laugh against her skin.

"Not so fast, wife," he taunted. "I am not ready to finish with you yet."

Elizabeth did scream then, for instead of filling her, he withdrew from her just when the ripples of pleasure and release threatened inside of her.

"Jamie!" she cried out. "Now!" He held her steady as he laid on the bed next to her.

"Ride me, lass."

He liked it when she climbed on him and was in

control of the pace and timing. He liked it because he could watch her face as she reached that final peak. He liked it because he could reach up and touch and suckle her breasts as she moved over him.

He especially liked it when she shuddered and shook through her release after he rubbed his fingers between their bodies in that place she liked. It was swollen now from his mouth using it and it would take only a touch or two to push her over her edge. She climbed over his groin as he lifted his cock and let her ease down on it.

From the tight fit, he knew it would take him little to explode within her. She pulled her knees in close to his hips and began the torture he so loved. Her hair fell like a silken curtain around her body. As she arched and moved, her nipples peaked through, inviting his touch there. Leaning up, he took one then the other in his mouth and suck it hard, grazing his teeth over the tip until he heard her breathing change.

The muscles within her core began to tighten and he knew his seed would be filling her at any moment. His flesh swelled thicker, and she pushed against him. Then he held her hips and thrust deep once and again and a third time until he exploded.

It was some moments before either one could speak or breathe. Elizabeth collapsed on his chest and James wrapped his arms around her. When their hearts calmed, he brought her to his side and drew the bedcovers up over them.

Mornings were colder now and frost greeted them most days. Winter would be on its way to these lands soon. He would not mind it this year for it would bring them closer to the birth of their first child.

James had noticed the changes in her body almost before she did, beginning with the ones to her nipples and breasts. Now, her waist thickened and soon she would be ripe and full of his child.

The child he wanted to be born in his home. He needed to try to make peace with his father...and with Connor first.

Though unsure of her welcome, she understood his need to return to his home and make things right with his parents. In these last few months, they had hidden in plain sight, remaining here in the village and working as any other married couple would. James was learning the skills of the blacksmith and Elizabeth kept house and cooked. The witch had lied about that—she was a skilled cook though he was certain her brother would disagree.

He'd seen Dougal a few times when he rode through the village on the earl's business, but he'd never drawn attention to himself. Through some of the villagers, he'd learned that Tavis had indeed claimed Ciara as his wife, even before learning of James's actions. If Connor had allowed it, there was hope that he would not object too much to his and Elizabeth's marriage.

And today was the day they would begin their journey back to discover the true situation.

"Beth, my love," he whispered to her. "We must get ready for our journey."

She mumbled something and rolled to her other side.

"Everything is packed and ready. It all waits only for us." She lifted her head and glanced at him.

"And you are ready to return?" she asked, sliding from the warmth of the bed and beginning to dress. "What do you think Connor will say?"

"He cannot pull us apart," he said, grabbing her hand and pulling her close. That was her biggest worry. "He allowed Ciara to marry Tavis—a good sign, that."

"What about your parents?"

"They will come to love you as I do. If they want their grandchild born in their home, and I think they will, they will accept us together." He kissed her as he stood next to her. "Oh, there will be some rough days, but with you at my side, we will get through it."

Within hours, they were on the road north and west toward the center of the MacLeries' lands and his main stronghold. More than that, they rode together into the life they'd been bold enough to claim for themselves.

Love, he thought, made everything simple.

Connor stood in his favorite place, watching the couple enter through the gates of Lairig Dubh. He knew who they were and knew they would arrive this morn. As he observed them, he took note of the way the younger man reached out to touch his wife's hand often as they rode to the keep. He saw how others in the yard caught sight of them and stopped to watch them go by.

Duncan and Rurik called out to him as they crossed the battlements to reach him. He waited for them before going into the hall to greet James Murray and his wife on their arrival here.

"You knew, did you not?" Duncan asked.

"I own the village. Of course, I knew," he answered. "The priest earns his living from my generosity. I knew when they arrived there, the trouble they had and knew when they married."

"And you did nothing to stop them?" Rurik asked, crossing his arms over his chest.

"We'd secured the agreements we wanted from his father based on his leaving Ciara at the altar. I agreed to pay Elizabeth's dowry since she is my kin. If the boy was bold enough to claim her in the old style, who am I to stop him?"

Connor laughed then, for neither one of his closest friends knew if he jesting with them or telling the truth. Or if his wife had just softened his heart to the plight of the young lovers. It mattered not, for everything had been settled in his favor and the results pleased him.

Elizabeth, who had faltered once before and had survived that had found a good husband in James Murray. A wedding between James and Ciara would have been a disaster, so his precipitous elopement had, in some ways, saved Connor's arse. Though he would never admit such to anyone.

Connor was about to head into the keep when a scream echoed across the yard and drew him to a stop. Ciara ran across the inner yard towards James and Elizabeth, screaming out the girl's name. She'd gotten a start ahead of Tavis, who followed her. Without realizing it at first, Connor held his breath, waiting to see how this encounter would go. The scream was not a good sign.

And, as he had been before, he was wrong once more.

Ciara reached them first and threw her arms around Elizabeth, hugging her and rocking side to side. She drew back, said something else to the lass and then they were both screaming and crying together. Tavis stopped a pace or two away and Connor could tell the moment that the two men involved saw each other.

One spoke to the other and back again and Connor could feel the tension even from his place high on the wall. Had he been wrong?

James held out his hand to Tavis, who took it without hesitation. Then Ciara hugged James as Elizabeth hugged Tavis.

"Well, as I said, it would all work itself out."

He turned and walked away, knowing that it had indeed all worked out. His wife would say it was all due to love, but she was softhearted, as most women were. He knew it was because they each made the right choices.

But, even the Beast of the Highlands knew he could be wrong once in a while. As he had been in this.

If you enjoyed *"The Forbidden Highlander"*,
don't miss *"The Highlander's Dangerous Temptation"*

This USA TODAY bestselling story involves Lady
Jocelyn's younger brother and Rurik's daughter in
another arranged marriage attempt by meddling parents.
In this scene, Athdar and Isobel are playing chess and it
leads to something… more.

*Please turn the page to enjoy an excerpt from*

# *The Highlander's Dangerous Temptation*

Athdar looked up and saw Isobel approaching. She walked quickly and decisively towards him. Padruig stood to leave, but he put his hand on Athdar's shoulder and squeezed.

"You do not stand a chance, my friend."

Athdar wanted to ask what he meant before Isobel got close enough to hear. Padruig laughed then, smacked his back and moved away.

"Lady," he said as he passed Isobel, "he mounts a strong defence, but dinna be fooled by it." Padruig warned her loud enough for Athdar to hear.

If Isobel was disturbed by it, she showed no sign of being so. Athdar dragged two chairs close together, near the warmth of the hearth. Isobel grabbed the small table and pulled it between them.

"You finished packing quickly," he said as he reached for the wooden box and game board. "I did not expect you for nigh on another hour or more."

"My mother said I was making a mess of things, so she told me to leave!"

He waited for her to sit and then did so. "I suspect you have used that tactic in the past with great success." Her cheeks took on a pale pink hue as she blushed, confirming his suspicions without answering. "Which colour would you like?"

"I like the black pieces," she said. Lifting one up, she wrapped her fingers around it and rubbed the edges of it. Athdar swore he felt her touch on the hard parts of his anatomy and tried not to show it. "The dark appeals to me."

Though he would die before doing anything dishonourable, he was thinking of many, many things he would like to do with her as he watched her caress the carved wooden figure. He shook himself free of desire's control and took up the red pieces, arranging them in lines on the board. With the way she'd played the first night, he needed his wits about him if he stood a chance of winning or even drawing a tie.

He allowed her the first move and it was not long before she began taunting him with risky moves, placing her pieces in harm's, or his, way. Athdar resisted the urge to fall for her feints. She would make a remarkable strategist in any battle or war, he thought, as she claimed yet another of his. It took losing nearly half of his 'army' before he saw her pattern. He laughed aloud when he did, finally seeing the simple way she tested and took or tested and retreated from a confrontation.

Then it was too late for him, so caught up in appreciating the intelligence of her play that he missed her final series of moves that took his queen, then his king. This time she laughed, too, along with him. A few of the servants still working in the hall turned at the sound of it.

"Another?" he asked, motioning at the main table for cups and a pitcher. Ailean saw it and brought them. Isobel glanced around the hall and then back at him.

"The polite thing for me to do is to beg off from another game, but I would like to continue," she answered.

"Then, let's," he said, with a motion of his hand to let her take the first move.

He'd learned much about her style of play and he was prepared for her this time. This game moved at a leisurely pace, each of them studying the board a bit longer than in the previous games. They'd taken several moves each, and he'd already lost a piece when she spoke.

"So, what do you call your keep?"

"The keep?" he said, looking up at her. "I have no name for it." He thought about it for a moment and then realised what she meant. "It is not big and grand enough to have a name."

"Oh, it is big enough. And you could make it grand, if you wanted it so," she said.

"Have you ever visited your grandfather's?" If she had, 'twas no wonder she thought of grander places—Rurik's father was the Earl of Orkney and one of the wealthiest men in Norway.

"I have met him, aye." She leaned in closer and lowered her voice so only he could hear it. "Father does not wish me to become accustomed to the way his father lives. But I have visited my grandmother in Caithness and stayed several months with her."

Her father's father had extraordinary wealth and power in the northern islands while her father's mother was a nun, supervising a convent in the north-east of Scotland—two extremes in life—and yet Isobel seemed no more impressed by one than the other.

"Your father is a practical man," he said.

Her eyes flashed and her cheeks turned bright red then. She laughed, leaning back against the chair and holding her stomach. She was so vibrant he thought the hall grew brighter from it. Only then did he notice that her hair was not bound up in a braid, but hanging loose and swirling around her as she moved.

"In all my years..."

He frowned at her. *All* her years?

"For as long as I can ever remember, you and my father have had nothing good to say about each other. Ever," she said, wiping her hand across her eyes. "I do not understand the basis for your animosity, though I have heard various rumoured bits of it.... That is the only good thing you have ever said about him."

Her laughter yet echoed through his hall and he wanted to hear it go on and on. For so long, this had been a place of sadness, and would be again, but for now, he enjoyed her mirth.

"I am certain I have said good things about him." Athdar searched his memory for that good thing now and could not bring it to mind. "I have admired his fighting skills."

She stopped laughing, but her mouth curved in the most appealing smile then. "So tell me how it happened. I would like to hear the truth of it."

Athdar hesitated. To put one's humiliation on display was not done easily. Yet...

"I was but ten-and-five and full of myself."

"As most young men are at that age," she added. She was much closer to that age than he was.

"I travelled through Lairig Dubh on my father's business and had the opportunity to watch your father in a fight with Connor. Apparently, it was a custom of theirs to engage in swordplay when they met up and I was witness to both their skill and strength. Scared the bravado right out of me."

He shifted in his chair, wondering how to tell her the rest of it. She was, after all, a young woman with certain sensibilities.

"I was a guest there and managed to get myself rather drunk one night at dinner. I insulted your father and found myself the victim, though at my own instigation, of his fury and his strength. I ended up with broken arms, nose and many, many bruises."

It was worse than that, truly. The worst was not the two broken arms or the other physical injuries. The worst was when he understood the situation he'd drawn the unsuspecting and unwilling Jocelyn into because of his youthful stupidity. Her dreams of marrying the man she loved were torn apart by his foolish, drunken challenge that put him in the custody of the Beast of the Highlands.

Rurik had visited him in the depths of Broch Dubh and told him exactly what he would cost Jocelyn. All because he could not control himself. All because he did not think of the consequences of his actions. Not unlike an earlier time when...

A memory flared and faded in that moment. Something dark and terrifying flitted across his memories and sank back into the murky depths from which it had risen. Nausea followed, then his head felt as though struck from behind.

"Athdar?"

His vision narrowed and then widened. He could hear only a buzzing in his ears. Then all of it began to fade away.

"Athdar?" Isobel said, caressing his face. When had she touched him? When had she risen from her chair and approached him? "Are you ill?" She crouched down closer before him and stroked his forehead and cheek with the back of her hand. "No fever."

"I am well," he said, though he was trying to convince himself of it more than her. "What happened?" He swallowed, but his mouth and throat were parched. She noticed and held out a cup to him.

"You were telling me of your confrontation with my father and then something happened. You looked as if in pain and then ill. Now?" she asked, taking the cup from him and kneeling next to him.

Strange. He had been thinking about the true humiliation of learning the unintended consequences that Jocelyn suffered when some other memories or feelings surged forwards. Now they were gone and he felt fine.

"'Tis a painful thing—exposing a man's youthful stupidity to a beautiful woman who is the daughter of the man who exposed it in the first place. You now know my sordid past with your father, Isobel."

Her hand still caressed his face and, with her kneeling at his side, it would be easy, oh so easy, to lean down and kiss the lips that tempted him so much. When she lifted her head and her mouth opened slightly, he did what he wanted to do.

Her lips were soft and warm against his and he could feel her heated breath against his mouth before he touched it with his. Athdar did not touch her, but she did not let go of his face, stroking it as he deepened the kiss by sliding his tongue along her lips until she opened to him.... For him.

God, but she was sweet.

He knew not when it happened, but his hand slid up and he tangled his fingers in her hair. Then he cupped her head, and held her against his mouth. His tongue felt the heat deep in her mouth and he tilted his head tasting her and kissing her. For a moment, he drew back, but she looked at him with such wonderment in her eyes, that he kissed her again and again and again.

"Isobel?" Margriet called out.

She pulled away and pushed up to her feet faster than she realised she could. Her mouth, her lips and tongue, tingled from the way he'd touched her, kissed her. Isobel lifted her hand to touch her mouth, but her mother's voice came again through the corner of the now-darkened hall.

"'Tis late and you need your rest for the journey."

Had her mother been watching? Had she seen...?

"Go, lass," Athdar said as he stood up and took a step away. "I will see you in the morn before you leave." His hand grazed hers as she turned from him and she fought the urge to hold him. "Sleep well," he whispered as she passed him.

Her body hummed with some kind of heat and every part of her felt alive and achy at the same time. But her mouth... Her mouth hungered for more. More of him. More of his mouth against hers. More...

## Meet Terri Brisbin

Award-winning and *USA Today* best-selling author, **Terri Brisbin** is a mom, a wife, grandmom! and a dental hygienist from southern NJ. Terri writes all sorts of sexy, compelling historical romances including those set in the medieval Highlands of Scotland, during times when the Vikings ruled and warred and in the Regency ballrooms of London and Edinburgh. Since she likes a glimmer of Celtic magic and myths, she's written paranormal historicals, time travel romances as well as a fantasy series. More than 3 million copies of her 50+ romance novels and novellas have sold in more than 25 countries and 20 languages around the world.

Her current and upcoming historical and paranormal/fantasy romances will be published by Oliver Heber Books, Dragonblade Publishing and Harlequin Historicals.

Connect with Terri:

Facebook: @TerriBrisbin

Facebook Author Page: @TerriBrisbinAuthor

Instagram: @TerriBrisbin

# *TerriBrisbin.com*

Made in the USA
Columbia, SC
02 March 2025

54607437R00085